THREE POUNDS OF

PRESSURE 2

WHEN PRESSURE IS

APPLIED

A Novel

By

Mike Curry

Front Cover Image by Unseen Handz Media
Book Design by Unseen Handz Media
Editor: Unseen Handz Media
First printing edition 2021 in the United States

Unseen Handz Media, LLC
1206 Motor Avenue
Helena, MT 59602

Acknowledgements

Peace!

I would like to give acknowledgements to all those who had supported me in the first two novels that I had published "3 Pounds of Pressure" and "Shattered Dreams". All the positive feedback I received means a lot to me. I would also like to give thanks to the Unseen Handz Media team for putting this together.

Thanks to my dawg Box, you was there from the beginning and rooted for me since day one. This is the one and you know how the story goes. I did this for us big homie. Treece, thanks for believing in me and helping me bring all these dreams into reality and to my brothers who support every move I make, it means the world to me.

Peace.

Dedication

Death is a hard pill to swallow especially when the love on both sides are mutual. I would like to dedicate this book to my cousin "Michael Shawn Curry" who passed away on August 18th 2021. You and I shared the same name but we also shared so many other qualities and a bond that no one can take from us. I love you cuz and your legacy will always live on through me and the rest of our family.

Rest In Peace

Chapter 1

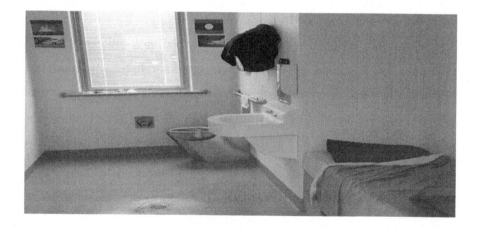

"Carter. It's your day. Pack up and meet me out in the dayroom," the staffer said, as he walked inside Scar's room.

Scar stepped off the bed and stared at his reflection in the mirror. His finger gently probed the scar on his left cheek. The scar was half-inch wide and started by his ear and went straight to his jawline creating a pear shape. The scar reminded him of the day that his cousin Faury crept up on him and sliced him from ear to mouth with a can opener. While in the custody of the Department of Youth Services Scar's father had sent him lessons from the Nation of Gods and Earths. Over the years Scar studied the lessons and saw that they applied to everything in life.

Uncle Stretch was part of the Nation of Gods and Earths. He took his teachings seriously. He gave his son the righteous attribute "Asiatic" and taught him what he had learned from his enlightener. The lessons gave Scar self-awareness, discipline and ways to show and prove facts. Even though Scar practiced righteousness he still was infatuated with the overall gangster lifestyle.

Over the years Scar grew eight-inches and now stood at six foot one, one hundred and eighty pounds. Scar grabbed his t-shirt and got dressed. He walked out into the dayroom with his bag and was relieved that he could now put his past behind him. Scar walked out of the building and saw his mother's purple BMW X5 and smiled. He was bombarded with the early morning summer heat. "Summer, summer time," he sang, as he walked over toward the BMW.

Scar's mother saw him coming out of the building, stepped out, ran over to him, hugged and kissed him. "Come on, I have to take you out to eat and then shopping. Throw all those old clothes in the trash." His mother said.

Scar grabbed his Nation of Gods & Earths lessons out of the bag, a few pictures and tossed the bag in the dumpster. He slid into the BMW and they rode off. Baby Fe took her son to get something to eat and then to the mall for shopping. After they shopped, they went to see his grandmother and a few other family members before heading to Norwood. While Scar was locked up his mother moved out of Academy homes and into a one-family house in Norwood Massachusetts. On their way home Scar studied the route she took to get there and noticed a commuter rail train station.

"Ma! Where's that train going?"
"To Boston." Baby Fe answered.

Scar remained quiet because that was all he needed to know. He was going to use the commuter rail back and forth to Boston until he had learned how to drive.

Baby Fe pulled up to the house and parked in the driveway. Scar stepped out, grabbed his bags and followed his mother into the house. He saw bags of clothes and appliances on the couch and tables.

"That is from your father, he said call him." Baby Fe said handing Scar a cell phone.
"Thanks." Scar said, as he dialed his father's number.
They spoke for less than an hour and Scar agreed to take a plane to the West Coast to see him before ending the call. He grabbed the bags of clothes and walked into the room. He pulled out some Adidas T-shirts,

3

sweatpants, tank tops and linen short sets.

"Damn, he sent me enough clothes to last the whole summer," Scar said, as he placed the clothes in his dresser and closet.
He spent the rest of the afternoon and evening with his mother before retiring for the night. The next morning Scar heard a knock on his door and jumped up.

"Are you ready to go to D.R.C.?" Baby Fe asked, peeking her head inside of the room.

The D.R.C. was short for Dorchester Resource Center. It was a program that juveniles that have been committed to the Department of Youth Services had to attend once released.

Scar got dressed and they left. Scar listened to music as they drove from Norwood to Boston. As his mother stopped at a red light in Codman Square Scar saw his man Murder from the Buck Shot Boys. "MURDER," Scar shouted from the window of the BMW.

Murder was outside of a McDonald's restaurant with a few of his goons. He heard a raspy voice shout his name and looked around. He saw someone waving a hand trying to get his attention. He saw that it was Scar waving and crossed the street.

Baby Fe pulled over in front of the D.R.C. and kissed her son. Scar stepped out and waited for Murder to join him. Murder came across

4

the street in a black and red Adidas T-shirt, black sweatpants, and a pair of red and black Adidas Sneakers.

"What's good," Murder said, extending his fist.
Scar gave him a pound and a hug. Murder and Scar became friends during their stay at the secure Treatment Center in Worcester Massachusetts.
"I have to do this Anger Management program," Scar said as he nodded to the building.
"Those programs be bullshit. When you finish I will be up the street at the Walgreens parking lot." Murder said, as he gave Scar a pound and walked across the street.

Scar stepped inside the building and the first person he saw was Monster from Orchard Park Housing Project. Scar felt chills run up his spine when he spotted Monster's Portland Trail Blazers Hat. They had met while they were serving time at the Worcester Secure Treatment Center. They never spoke until one day when Monster seen Scar's Atlanta Braves T-shirt. Upon seeing the t-shirt Monster laughed and told Scar that the A on the shirt was used for target practice in Orchard Park. Scar felt disrespected then and now.

Monster saw Scar, gave him the middle finger salute, and walked over to him. He looked down on the shorter Scar, "I should fuck you up," Monster snarled, as he lifted his Portland Trail Blazers hat up a few inches.
"You are not going to fuck nothing up." Scar said.

5

"Shut up little Nigga. I'll smack you out here in these streets. Play around lay around bitch." Monster said grilling Scar.

A few caseworkers walked over and separated the two. They grilled each other for a few seconds and went separate ways.

Scar knew right then and there that the next time he came to the program that he would bring a gun or a knife. He finished up his session and walked up the street where Murder was hanging.

Murder saw Scar walking toward him and motioned him across the street to a Chinese food restaurant. They stepped inside the Chinese restaurant and Murder ordered a box of spare ribs. They sat down at a table in the corner and started to talk.

"You want some of these spare ribs?" Murder asked.
"Nah! I don't fuck with that pork shit." Scar said.

Murder's attention was diverted by a light tap on the window. Murder saw a dope fiend and walked outside.

Scar Watched Murder exchange something with a drug addict. A few seconds later Murder came back and sat down. "What you getting money?" Scar asked.
"Yeah! There's no money like Dope Money." Murder said looking Scar in the eyes 'are you trying to get paper?'"
"Nah!" Scar answered, "I just had words with Monster from Orchard

Park."

"Yeah! You, know he's out here smacking niggas left and right." Murder informed.

"Smacking what you mean by that?" Scar asked, remembering how Monster threatened to smack him.

"Murdering niggas. He's a top flight gangsta out here in these streets. You can hate all you want on him but you have to respect how he handles his business. If you're beefing with that nigga you have to stay toned up and bring your A-game."

"Toned?" Scar was confused about what tone meant.

"Yeah! Tone means a strap my nigga."

"Oh! There's going to come a time when you're going to need paper to finance wars. You can't win any war without having paper. Remember that. When you ready you know where I'm at." Murder said, as he fell into a nod.

Scar watched Murder fall into a deep nod and thought he fell asleep. He watched as Murder came out of the nod and started eating his spare ribs. Murder gave Scar a few more jewels and they left the restaurant and walked down Washington Street. Murder was still AWOL from the Department of Youth Services.

"Do D.Y.S. still be fucking with you?" Scar asked.

"Fuck them. They know what's up. When they see me, they know better to say anything to me or try to run up on me. All they do is just stare. I give them the middle finger salute and keep on moving." Murder replied.

"Damn, that's gangster," Scar said. "What bus goes to Ruggles

Station?"

"The bus you are looking for is the number Twenty-two. You see that bus stop?"

Murder pointed, "That's where you will get on the bus dog."

They walked to the bus stop and waited. A few minutes later the bus pulled up. Scar gave Murder the three-finger handshake and stepped on the bus. The bus drove past Academy Homes. Scar looked out the window and saw a half a dozen teenagers wearing Atlanta Braves caps and jerseys standing on Columbus Avenue. He smiled and mumbled, "I'll see y 'all tomorrow."

Chapter 2

The sound of his cousin Faury woke him up. He sat up in his bed. *"These nightmares have to stop,"* Scar thought, as he picked up his phone and saw that a whole day passed since he was released from juvenile detention. He got off the bed, walked downstairs and ate the breakfast his mother prepared before she went to work. After he ate, he took a shower, got dressed and then left. He walked to the commuter rail train station and sat on a bench. Fifteen minutes later his train pulled up, he stepped on and found a seat. As the train made its way to Ruggles Train Station he reflected on the conversation he had with his father before he was arrested and how he had lied about what really happened.

"I have to go to Arizona to see my dad ASAP." Scar said as he thought about what led him to spend the last five years in the Department of Youth Services.

The commute from Norwood to Academy homes was a little less than an hour. Scar had to use the commuter rail train system from Norwood to Ruggles' Bus and Train Station, and then boarded a city bus to Academy Homes. This was his first time returning to his housing projects since age eleven. The bus stopped and Scar stepped off. Scar was dressed in a charcoal gray linen short set and gray Top Ten Adidas. He looked at the buildings that made up Academy homes, swallowed his spit, walked across the street and into the project.

Scattered around the courtyard were groups of people playing dice, hustling and drinking beer. He walked toward a crowd of niggas his age.

"Peace," Scar greeted the group.

"Who you?" A youngster named Little Barry asked, stepping forward.

Scar knew mathematics never lied. He held his guard and looked at all the unfamiliar faces and said Peace again. Scar knew his family's name held weight in the project and around the city and he wasn't going to let a negative force outweigh the positivity that existed within him. He saw the look on the youngsters faces and decided to make his presence known. He knew in order to get the results he wanted he had to come to the people as the people.

"My name is Scar. I'm from out here. I used to live over there on Weaver Way." He replied, as he pointed to his old building on Weaver Way.

"I been around here all my life and I don't remember you. Who's your peeps? Name some names?" Another youngster named Red asked as he lifted his shirt to reveal the handle of a Ruger P89.

Scar wasn't ready to reveal who his father was because he intended to carve his own reputation in the project. He knew if he tried to be brave that he would be left where he was standing.

"My father is Stretch." Scar answered.

"Uncle Stretch?" Red asked, as he let his shirt drop over the gun

"Yeah! That's my dad," Scar said.

A stocky nigga wearing a throwback Dale Murphy Jersey stepped forward, "okay, I remember you now. You were all over the news when you were a little kid. You just now coming home from that shit."

"Yeah!" Scar said.

"He's official tissue. Let me introduce you to the team dawg," Pitt said, as he reached and gave Scar the three-finger handshake. "This is Red, Little Barry, Homicide and I am Pitt. "So, they call you Scar huh?"

"Yeah! The name is Scar," Scar answered, as he turned his face to the side to show the pear-shape scar on his left cheek.

"Welcome home nigga. Where's your Atlanta Braves cap at?"

"I don't have one. Scar answered.

"Well, you need one to rep around here. What time is it? Pitt asked.

"It's a quarter past twelve," Little Barry informed.

"It's still early. Come on," Pitt said, as he led the way to the project Bodega. "Over the years a lot of niggas got hurt fucking with us. Some shot, stabbed, beat down and even killed. You see that project across the street," he pointed to Bromley Heath Street.

"Yeah! Scar said.

"We been at war with them since the beginning of time. That's one of our rivals. Watch out for this nigga named Bones he is a wild nigga.

13

He's at the top of our murder list."

A black Range Rover pulled up to the curb. A light skin, chubby older head with long cornrows that reached the bottom of his neck stepped out with a throwback Hank Aaron Jersey.

"Who is that?" Scar asked.

"Yo! That's Free. He's an older head from the Light Side." Pitt said.

"The Light Side, where is that? Scar asked.

"There's two sides of the project. The Light Side and the Dark Side. The Washington Street and Codman Park area is the Light Side and this area where we hang out is called the Dark Side." Pitt informed.

"Oh! Okay." Scar said, as Free made his way up the stairs and into the crowd. He stopped at Scar and saw that Scar had no Atlanta Braves hat on.

"Where are you from?" Free asked.

"The A." Scar replied.

"I never saw you around here. Who are you and what's your name little nigga?" Free asked.

"I used to live on Weaver Way. Tthey call me Scar." Scar answered.

"That's Uncle Stretch's son," Little Barry said.

"Oh yeah! Where's your daddy at? He still hiding in Arizona?" Free laughed.

Scar felt disrespected by the line of questioning and the manner how Free approached him. He looked at Pitt and back at Free.

"I see he got game. I'll be sure to tell my father what you said." Scar said sarcastically.

"Tell him. No-one's scared of him. Since you talk tough and act tough, to be around here you have to put in work, little nigga. Someone give this nigga a hammer. He's going across the street to handle his business. That's your initiation little nigga," Free said, pointing to Bromley-Heath Street Project.

"Nah! That's not a good look. Don't you see all those police cruisers across the street." Pitt cut in.

Scar gave Free a devious smile. In time, he knew Free was going to be a problem that needed to be handled. He didn't know when, but he knew it would be soon.

Free stepped off and made his way back to his Range Rover. He sat in the driver's seat for a while staring at Scar. He still remembered the day when Uncle Stretch shot him three times and now that Scar was back in the project Free would use Scar to bring Uncle Stretch back to town. He put the Range Rover in drive, pulled off and headed down the street.

"You good?" Red asked.

"Yup." Scar replied."

"That's Free. He held the project down for years," Red said patting Scar on his shoulder.

"Let's go and get some more troops, head downtown and get him his Atlanta Braves hat," Pitt said.

They walked to the Four Squares, rounded up six more people and walked to Stony Brook Train Station. They hopped on the train. Everyone had on different types of Braves hats except Scar. He felt like an outcast. This was Scar's first time in the midst of some real gangsters. His adrenaline pumped as he was ready to prove himself. He eyed a few pretty girls as they boarded the train.

"Yo! You want to hold the heat?" Little Barry asked.

"Yeah!" Scar said calmly.

"Come on," Homicide said, as he walked to the back of the train.

When they reached the back of the train Little Barry reached in his waist, pulled out the bulky .9mm and passed it to Scar. An older lady watched the exchange, shook her head and turned away. She couldn't understand why the younger generation was so infatuated with killing one another. Scar walked back to where the rest of the crew was posted and took a seat. A couple of stops later the train stopped at Jackson Square.

Jackson Square was home to their rivals, Bromley Heath Street. They all stood on their seats looking to see if they saw any Miami Heat hats. Five stops later, they stepped off the train at Downtown Crossing and headed toward the store. They walked into a hat store and studied the Atlanta Braves' caps. Scar stared at a gray Braves cap that matched his linen short set.

"Pick one." Pitt said.

Scar pointed to the gray Atlanta Braves cap. Pitt bought the cap and watched as Scar tossed it on his head.

"I love it." Scar said looking in the mirror. They walked out of the store. As they crossed the street, they saw a bunch of niggas flooding the street and sidewalk wearing Cleveland Cavaliers caps. "Who's those niggas?" Scar asked.

"That's C.V.O. (Cape Verdean Outlaws). Their whole crew is Cape Verdeans. They be up on the Bowdoin and Hamilton area," Pitt said, as he threw up his fist to his man Sauce Money.

Pitt opened the door to Expressions Clothing Store and walked in. Scar saw over a dozen Cape Verdeans with Washington Nationals' Caps on. He knew from his travels in the juvenile system that Wendover Street wore the caps, and that they were having a bloody war with C.V.O..

"SCAR!" a Wendover Street Gang member named Rocky shouted.

Scar turned around and saw Rocky. He walked up to him and gave him a hug. They spoke briefly and then rejoined their circles.

"I see those Mission Hill niggas are deep," Pitt said, as he stared at the pack of Michigan Wolverine caps near the sneaker section. Scar reached in his waist for the Ruger. He was ready to squeeze and clear the store out. "Nah! Not here. We aren't at war with them," Pitt informed.

17

Scar listened to Pitt and walked toward the Adidas section. He picked up a pair of blue, red, and white Top Ten Adidas. "How much?" Scar asked.

"Eighty-five dollars," The sales lady said.

Scar paid for the sneakers, a T-shirt and some jeans. They walked out of the store and hopped on the train back to the hood. They made it back to the project with no problems. As soon as they stepped in the courtyard, they saw Free in front of a building with a few older heads. Free saw them and made his way toward the pack of youngsters. He stopped at Scar and reached for the bag.

"What's in the bag?" Free asked.

Scar moved the bag away. Free flipped Scar's Atlanta Braves cap off his head onto the ground. Scar dropped the bag and reached for his waist. Free saw Scar clutching his waist and laughed.

"I wish you would new jack. Remember that you're a new jack around here." Free said, "don't forget to tell your daddy to come out of hiding." Little Barry grabbed Scar by the waist and pulled him back. Pitt stepped in the middle and pushed Free back. "Don't touch me little nigga," Free barked. "I will spank that little nigga in this courtyard and dump his body in that dumpster" Free said pointing to Scar and then the dumpster.

"You wish," Scar responded, as he picked up his cap, brushed it off, and tossed it on his head.

"You're a punk-like your daddy," Free said, as he walked away from the crowd.

"This nigga got me fucked up, I'm going to have to kill him quick, fast and in a hurry," Scar thought, as he saw a Mercedes-Benz S-class pull up into the parking lot. He watched as a slim built, brown skin nigga step out with an Atlanta Braves cap.

"Yo! Pitt. Who's that?" Scar asked.

"That's the nigga Riot. He's part of our circle. He was raised in St. Joe's, but he reps the A."

"Oh! I was in juvey with a few niggas from St. Joes." Scar said.

"He's a good nigga. He's touching some decent paper out here too." Pitt said.

"I can see," Scar said, as he stared at Riot's chain.

Riot walked over and gave dap to Pitt and when he reached Scar, he introduced himself and stuck out three fingers. Scar gave him the three-finger handshake.

"I like that A hat," Scar said.

"I try to get all the flavors that niggas can't find." Riot said, "What you new to the hood?"

"Yeah and No! I'm originally from out here, but I had been in juvie for a while."

"That's what's up. When you come home?" Riot asked.

"The other day."

"Okay." Riot said, as he reached in his pocket and pulled out a knot of money, peeled off a few bills and passed it to Scar.

"Good look," Scar said, as he took the money and put it in his pocket.

"There's no need to thank a gee. Real niggas do real things. We going to get up. Let me make these runs," Riot said as he gave dap and walked away.

Scar thoughts reverted to how disrespectful Free was. *"Don't this nigga know that it only takes three pounds of pressure to pull a trigger."* Scar thought.

Chapter 3

Scar followed Pitt and the rest of the crew through the courtyard and stopped near a set of railings.

Scar leaned against the railings, tilted his Atlanta Braves Cap to cover his face. The only thing on his mind was how he was going to kill Free.

A pretty light-skinned female approached the crowd in a lime green Puma, velour sweat suit. She stopped and held a brief conversation with Pitt. Scar saw Pitt look his way and then motioned him to join them. The female that Pitt was talking to was known throughout the project as "Strawberry" for the light freckles that covered her face. At 24 years old she was a professional crack abuser and one of the youngest prostitutes in the project. She kept her body tight even though she abused crack. Sucking and fucking was how she got high.

Scar stepped up and followed them to a building on Ritchie Street. She used her key to open the door and walked straight to the bedroom. She stopped, turned around and reached out her hand. Pitt spit a twenty rock of crack out his mouth and handed it to her. She inspected it like a food inspector and then walked deeper into the room. Pitt pushed Scar to follow her.

"Get your dick wet nigga," Pitt said with a smile on his face.

Scar hesitated and then joined her in the room. Strawberry kicked off her sneakers, pulled down her sweatpants, and leaned over. Scar saw how meaty her pussy was. He quickly unbuttoned his pants and pulled out his dick.

"I need a condom," Scar blurted out.

Strawberry turned around and grabbed a blue Durex Condom from the dresser and ripped it open with her teeth. She sat on the edge of the bed and placed the condom on his dick. She grabbed his dick with her left hand, wrapped her lips around it and started giving him a blow job. She gave him a good five minutes of head and then stopped. "It's time for you to get some of this pussy." She said and then scooted backward onto the bed and spread her legs.

Scar slid on the bed and placed his dick inside of her. He grabbed her legs, hoisted them on his shoulders, and started pumping with deep strokes. He noticed how loose her pussy was and continued stroking. After fifteen minutes of stroking he filled the condom with cum and pulled out. He climbed off the bed, pulled off the condom, and went into the bathroom to clean himself.

Scar finished cleaning himself, stepped out of the bathroom and saw Strawberry cleaning a stem in the living room. She looked up and spotted Scar staring at her.

"Thank you. Anytime you need me you know where to find me cutie. What's your name?" Strawberry asked.

"Scar."

"Alright Scar, thanks for the good time," Strawberry said, as she winked at Scar.

"*I should be thanking you for breaking my virginity,*" Scar thought.

"I'll see you later," Scar said to Strawberry, as he stepped toward the living room where Pitt was waiting.

"Ole Strawberry done broke my nigga's virginity," Pitt joked, "Let's get out of here before this bitch asks for another dub."

They left Strawberry's apartment and walked to Academy Court where the rest of the crew were in the courtyard hustling.

"BUY THREE AND GET ONE FREE," Homicide advertised to a

crackhead.

"Later, honey." a toothless crackhead said.

"Let's go to my girl Kia's apartment," Pitt said, as he led the way across the courtyard.

Scar, Gangster and Hood followed him to an apartment on Slayton Way. Pitt opened the door and stepped in and walked into a bedroom. Gangster and Hood raced to the living room and snatched the X- box controllers. A few minutes later a petite female stepped out of the bedroom with Pitt wearing an oversized Atlanta Braves' T-shirt.

Kia was one of the prettiest females in the project. She had long curly hair that she kept in a bun. She had a son named Kewaun that she had named after her baby's father who was killed in a shoot-out a few years earlier outside of Jackson Square MBTA station.

"What's your name?" Kia asked.

"Scar."

"My name is Kianna, but you could call me Kia."

"That's Uncle Stretch's son," Pitt said, as he passed Scar three gang-affiliated T-shirts.

Scar looked at the shirts and read the words.

"What's this a new clothing label?" Scar asked.

"Nah! That's the name of this record label that niggas be fucking with," Pitt answered.

"Who be rapping?" Scar asked.

"A few niggas in the project formed a group called Triple Threat and got a little buzz in the city," Pitt said, as he stepped behind Kia and placed his hands over her flat stomach.

Kia felt more at ease that Scar was homegrown and not a "cling-on." She respected all the good things that Uncle Stretch did for the project. She was a little girl when he gave free turkeys for Thanksgiving, U-Haul Trucks of toys for Christmas, and R&B Cruises on Mother's Day for all the single mothers in the project.

"My house is your home." Kia said to Scar.

Scar lifted his Atlanta Braves cap and showed his uni brow. He looked down at Kia's fingernails and noticed they had the Atlanta Braves logo painted on them. "Thank you," Scar said.

"There's no need to thank me, you are part of the family. I know you are coming to Academy Day?" Kia asked.

"What's Academy Day?" Scar asked.

"It's an annual cook-out that is held at Marcella Park every Fourth of July." Pitt said, as he thought about what happened a few years back at the cook-out when Juicy from Heath Street was killed. "Just make sure you are strapped because anything can happen there."

"Oh yeah! I'll be strapped and I will definitely be there." Scar confirmed.

"It was nice meeting you Scar. Make yourself at home." Kia said, as she walked into the bedroom with Pitt.

"Give me a minute dog." Pitt said. He spent about an hour in the room with Kia before he had come back to the living room. "Let's go down Eggie," Pitt said, as he walked to the front door.

They stepped outside of Kia's apartment and walked toward Columbus Avenue. Pitt wanted to show Scar a few people who would one day become instrumental to him.

"You want a line-up dawg?" Pitt asked.

"Yeah!"

"Wait till you see these two fine ass sisters who work at Lawsons Barbershop. These bitches are bad. You are going to love them. Are you still strapped?"

Scar lifted his shirt revealing the Ruger. P89 tucked in his waistband.

"I'm strapped to." Pitt said, lifting his shirt showing Scar a blue steel .44 Revolver.

They walked to Egleston Square and saw a dozen niggas wearing Oakland Athletics Baseball caps in front of a pizza shop.

"Who's all them niggas?" Scar asked pointing to the group with the Oakland Athletics caps.

"That's them Light Side niggas. You see the one wearing the Jose Canseco Jersey?"

"Yeah! The pretty boy?"

"Yeah! That's Curly. He's a problem. Just last summer alone he caught four niggas slipping and twisted their shit back." Pitt informed, "Come on, let's go and holler at them."

They walked over to them and Pitt introduced Scar to each one. Scar shook their hands and looked at Curly and wondered what hood were the four niggas from he had killed last summer. After Pitt introduced Scar to them they turned and walked into the barbershop. Soon as they walked inside the barbershop Scar noticed a brown skin, thick female cleaning her clippers.

"Hey Tanya, how are you?"
"I'm good Pitt, how are you?" Tanya said, as she eyed Scar. She stared at him like she knew him from somewhere. "Who's your friend?"
"This is my nigga Scar."
"Hi Scar," Tanya said, as she reached over and grabbed a styling cape and a neck strip.
"Hi," Scar greeted.

Pitt sat down in her chair and waited for her to wrap the cape around his neck. Tanya wrapped the cape around him and placed a neck strip around his thick neck.

Scar stared at Tanya and agreed with Pitt about how pretty she was. He turned around and was struck by the beauty of a slimmer female with similar looks. She walked past with a bob cut, caramel skin and perfect facial features. She reminded him of the actress Halle Berry. Tia caught Scar staring at her and smiled.

"Hi! May I help you?" Tia asked.
"Tia, that's my nigga Scar give him a line-up." Pitt said.

28

Scar took off his Atlanta Braves Cap and placed it on the styling station. He sat down in the barber's chair and waited for Tia to line him up.

"Damn, you have some long ass braids," Tia said, "Tanya, look how long his braids are." She said, as she turned the chair toward her sister. Tanya stopped cutting Pitt's hair and looked at Scar's braids.

"Damn, nigga what you Spanish?" Tanya said joking.

"Nah. I been growing my hair for the past ten years."

Tia wrapped the cape around Scar. Before she started he asked her to face him to the door of the Shop. Tia spun the chair around as Scar requested. He pulled the gun from his waist and placed it on his lap. He heard too many stories of people getting murdered inside barbershops and he wasn't taking no chance of him getting caught slipping.

"How old are you"? Tia asked.

"Eighteen."

"Oh! You're a baby. I never seen you before are you new around here?"

"Nah! I was in jail most of my life." Scar answered.

"Boy! You're still a baby. What jail was you in?" Tia asked.

"The Department of Youth Services. I was committed since I was Twelve years old."

"Damn, what you killed someone?" Tia said joking.

Scar didn't respond and stared at the cars passing by the shop. Tia finished his line-up and pulled off the cape. She saw Scar stuffing a gun in his waist and shook her head.

"These young boys are so trigger happy these days." Tia said to herself.

Scar stepped up and waited for Pitt in the waiting area. After Tanya finished Pitt's hair he paid for both cuts and they left.

"I told you them sisters were pretty," Pitt said, as they walked back to the project.

"Pretty is an understatement," Scar said, as he gave Pitt dap, "The one who did my line-up looks like a younger version of Halle Berry. I like that bitch. She's a dime."
"Yeah! Tia is a dime piece," Pitt agreed.

They walked to the project and saw a group of older niggas talking.

"Yo! You met Cash yet?"
"Nah! Who's that?" Scar asked.
"He used to run with your pops back in the days."
"Oh Alright," Scar said, as he walked toward the crowd.

They approached the crowd and Scar was introduced to a few older heads and saw that one of them had a C.G. on his neck.

30

"What's up Scar. I have been looking for you. Your moms told me you were down here." Said the one with the tattoo on his neck.

Scar looked at him and wondered where he knew him from. He looked closer and remembered who he was. "They call you Trigga right?" Scar asked.

"Yeah! That's me. Damn, little nigga you almost as tall as me. You remember Nice?" Trigga said, as he pointed to Nice.

"I think so. He looks familiar." Scar said.

"What's up little nigga? Welcome home. I'm really good friends with your parents. I told your dad that I'll look out for you." Nice said, as he stared at Scar. *"Damn, the little nigga looks just like Uncle Stretch."* Nice thought.

"What are you doing?" Trigga asked.

"Nothing." Scar answered.

"Come on. Let's go shopping and get you some gear." Nice said.

Scar gave Pitt and the older heads from his project dap and left with Nice and Trigga. They drove straight to the mall and bought Scar a few outfits, sneakers and then took him around Castlegate and introduced him to everyone in the hood. Scar felt at home around Castlegate and decided to split his time between hanging on Castlegate and in his project.

*

Chapter 4

Scar woke up the next morning with a light tap from his mother. "Good morning baby, if you need any money or any more clothes just ask me. I'm about to go to work I'll see you later." Fesal said.

Scar's mother's side of the family was from Castlegate and those who knew her called her Baby Fe in honor of an O.G. from that hood name Big Fe.

Scar thought about his life, the direction he wanted to go in and the nigga Monster. He knew the next time he saw Monster that the encounter wouldn't be friendly. He reached under his pillow and pulled out the gun that Homicide gave him. He raised the gun to his lips and kissed it. "It only takes three pounds of pressure to pull this bad boy," Scar said, as he placed the gun back under the pillow.

While Scar was in the department of Youth Services, he spoke to his mother numerous times about continuing his education on a college level. He knew whatever he put his mind to he would succeed. Scar decided within the next few days that he would sign up for financial aid and enroll in a community college for the Fall Semester. He heard a knock on his door. He grabbed the gun from underneath his pillow and stashed it under his bed. He walked to the door, looked through the peephole and saw his caseworker. "Fat bitch," Scar mumbled, as he opened the door, "good morning Ms. Acres" Scar greeted.

"Good morning Mr. Carter," Ms. Acres said, as she waddled inside the apartment and sat on the couch.

Ms. Sherry Acres was considered the worst caseworker in the Department of Youth Services. She never met a juvenile that she liked and Scar wasn't an exception.

"It's eight in the morning what made you stop by?" Scar asked.

"I came by to check to see if you had made any progress searching for employment."

"I have only been out a week. The past week I have been with my family. I ain't really have no time to do too much."

"Well, you need to start. Because I would hate to pull you back in until your twenty-first birthday." She threatened.

"Are you serious? Don't worry. If I don't have a job by the end of the summer then I would be enrolled in college."

"Well, we are in June and I advise you to start looking for a job or enroll in college. I'm giving you until September."

"That's three months," Scar said, as he looked at his caseworker in the eyes.

"I know. That's more than enough time to get your career started."

"I'll try my hardest," Scar said sarcastically.

"How is the anger management program? Is it helping you control that anger of yours?"

"Anger. I don't have anger issues. It's pointless for me to participate in that program." Scar replied.

"Pointless! Did you forget that you spit in my supervisors face three years ago?"

"No!"

"I hope not."

"Why do I have to go to the program two times a week?"

"That's the first phase of the program. After the first phase then you will enter phase two then you will only have to go once a week." Ms. Acres answered.

"I hate this ugly bitch," Scar thought, as he stared at his caseworker. "How do you expect me to go to this program two times a week if I find employment or enroll in school?"

"We will talk when that happens. I just came by to check on you and see your progress. I will stop by in a few weeks to see how you are doing Mr. Carter. Remember that September is the deadline." Ms. Acres threatened.

"Okay." Scar said as he watched Ms. Acres waddle out of the

apartment. Scar walked to his bedroom, grabbed one of the gang-affiliated T-shirts that Pitt gave him, a pair of Top Ten Adidas and his Atlanta Braves cap. He walked out of his apartment and toward the commuter rail train station.

"I have to do something to get this bitch off my back," Scar thought, as he sat on the bench and waited for his train. The train pulled up and he stepped on.

On his way to Boston Scar decided to go to Bunker Hill Community College and sign up for financial aid. He took the train to Charlestown and stepped off and walked to Bunker Hill Community College. He signed up for financial aid and decided to spend the next few days learning the streets of Boston. He figured if he was going to be part of the streets then he had to know the streets like the back of his hand. Scar decided to stay away from two of the city's deadliest housing projects.

The two housing projects that Scar decided to stay away from was Bromley-Heath Street and Orchard Park. He wasn't scared or afraid, he was smart. He knew if he ran into Orchard Park's top dog "Monster" or Bromley-Heath Street's "Bones", it would be instant drama.

Monster was the undisputed top dog in Orchard Park. He carried his housing project on his back. In the past three weeks he had murdered three people raising his total to five this year. He was sitting on a high horse and nobody could knock him off it. Scar had learned that Monster was close friends with Bones and going against the two would be a task that he believes he can handle on his own. The beef with Scar and Bones went back when Bones assaulted Scar in juvenile detention six years ago. Since then Scar hated Bones, Bromley-Heath Street and anyone associated with him or his project. Scar knew with them both being on the street that it was only a matter of time before they bumped heads.

Scar stepped off the train and got on the bus. The bus he was on pulled into Dudley Station and Scar saw Monster and a few members of his gang standing outside of a Chinese restaurant called "Yum-Yums". Scar stared at them from the window, he wanted to hop off and put a few hot ones in Monster, but he decided to wait. The bus pulled off and Scar knew that the next time he saw Monster that it would be gun-play. The bus pulled up to Grove Hall and Scar stepped off and walked to Castlegate.

He saw all the gangsters posted on the corner in front of the bodega wearing bright red Cincinnati Reds' caps. He approached and gave each of them pounds.

"What's popping nigga?" Ave said with a neck full of gold.
"You know just stopping by showing some love." Scar said as he watched a pretty female with slanted eyes step inside the bodega.
"Where are you coming from dawg?" Grouch asked, as he rested his

left foot on the stoop and cleaned his Adidas with his thumb.

"I just came from the crib." Scar answered.

"What's good with those Triple Threat niggas. I see you are wearing your gang-affiliated T-shirt. We need to link and do a few tracks. I'm telling you this Criminal Asylum shit is going to be the most talked-about C.D. this summer," Ave said.

"I don't know. I haven't met any of them niggas yet since I been out," Scar said as he watched a beautiful female with slanted type Chinese eyes step out of the bodega with a blunt in her hand.

"What's up niggas," Noodles said, as she reached and gave each nigga the Three Finger salute.

Noodles was half Japanese and black. Her stringy hair was concealed under a pink polo hat. She had on white capri pants and a pink t-shirt that had airbrushed Rest in Peace "Day-Day" in white lettering. Her white Adidas Gazelles had pink stripes. Her tattoo on her left ankle had C.G.G. (CastleGate Girls) in cursive.

Noodles was the prettiest female that Scar had ever seen. He looked her up and down and admired her style.

"Dam, this bitch looks like Karruche Tran." Scar thought.

"Hi. I'm Noodles." Noodles said as she gave Scar a hug.

"My name is Scar,"

"You from the A?" Noodles asked as she stared at Scar's T-shirt and Atlanta Braves cap.

"Yeah!" Scar answered.

"That's what's up. What side are you from?"

"The Dark Side." Scar answered.

"The Lion's Den," Noodles giggled, as she passed Grouch the blunt.

Grouch cracked the blunt, tossed the insides on the ground, and rolled up a twenty bag of weed into the blunt. He passed the rolled up blunt to Noodles. She sparked it, took a few puffs, and let it rotate. Ave swung the blunt to Scar. He declined and passed it to Noodles.

"You don't smoke?" Noodles asked.

"Nah!" Scar answered.

"That's weird. You don't catch too many people these days who don't smoke." Noodles said, as she finished the rest of the blunt.

"Yo, let's get something to eat" Ave said.

They all rose from the stairs and walked toward the pizza shop. Noodles broke off and headed toward a group of females who sat on the stairs.

"Peace, I'm off with my bitches now." Noodles said.

Scar looked at Noodles' perfect derriere and knew he had to have her one day. They turned the corner and Scar saw a rust orange BMW parked outside of the pizza shop. He stared and saw a crack fiend cleaning the BMW. He followed Ave and Grouch inside the pizza shop and was greeted by more members of the Castlegate gang.

Streets sat at a table on the phone surrounded by three pretty females. Streets was "the man" in the hood. Over the years he took his older cousin's (Nice) advice and became one of the top money makers in the hood. It showed by all the material possessions he had. Streets threw up the three-finger salute to Scar and kept staring out the window as the crack head cleaned his BMW.

Streets was the man on Castlegate. Besides Nice and Trigga he was the one to see for cocaine. He held the block down as he supplied guns and drugs to those in his circle. He also held down those in prison especially his best friend Raw Raw. Every week he sent Raw Raw money and pictures. He made sure at least once a month he drove to Otisville, New York and spent the day in the visiting hall with his best friend. He knew that Raw Raw's time in prison was getting short and in a few more years they would be on the streets getting money like the old days. Grouch walked up to Streets and sat down.

"What's good?" Streets asked.
"It's been slow out here, but here-go a stack for an onion" Grouch said passing Streets a thousand dollars.

These days, Streets only cared about four things: his money, bitches, his BMW and the well-being of his man Raw Raw.

Chapter 5

Streets got up from his seat in the pizza shop and walked over toward Scar. "What's up Scar? I heard you were out. Look at you nigga all big and shit looking like your daddy." Streets said as he gave Scar a hug. "I heard you came through the other day."

"Yeah I swung through here. Your cousin Nice and Trigga brought me around here and introduced me to everyone. What's up with you? I see you out here looking like a million bucks," Scar said, as he looked at the jewelry that Streets had on.

"I'm just getting this paper. When you ready to eat holler at me. What are you trying to do out here?"

"I'm just analyzing a few options. Thinking about going to school for something."

"I hear that. Make sure you take some sort of financial classes, so you know how to stack your money. It's a lot of money out here but if you don't know what to do with it, what's the sense of having it. If you need anything, you know where to find me," Streets said looking Scar in the eyes. "If I am not around here then I'm only a phone call away," Street said, as he reached in his pocket and pulled out a knot of bills. He peeled off a few fifty-dollar bills and passed them to Scar, "this is you dog. Always know that Castlegate is your second home."

"I already know that. Good looking out on the bread," Scar said, as he put the money in his pocket.

"Anytime. Money is nothing. I have plenty of it. Did you get some pussy yet?"

"Yeah!" Scar said.

"These little bitches these days are thirsty and will do anything for money." Streets said.

"I see." Scar said, thinking about Strawberry.

"All you need is a few ride or die bitches and you good. What's your plans for the day?" Streets asked.

"I'm about to hop on the bus and go to this anger management program. They got me going to this bullshit program."

"The bus. Niggas don't ride the bus, my nigga. Don't you know niggas be getting killed on them shits? I'll take you there," Streets said, as he walked toward the door of the pizza shop.

They walked out of the pizza shop and toward Streets BMW. He pulled a few twenty-dollar bills and paid the crack head for cleaning his car. He popped the lock and hit the automatic start.

"You ready," Streets said, as the engine roared.
"Yeah!" Scar said, as he opened the door and slid in the passenger seat to the fresh scent of pine.
"*It smells good,*" Scar thought, as he reclined the seat.

Streets put the car in drive and pulled off. He looked and saw that Scar was in deep thought and wondered what he was thinking about.

"What's on your mind dawg?" Streets asked.

Scar couldn't get Noodles out of his head.
"Yo! What's up with the chick Noodles?"
"Why you like her?" Streets asked.
"She's pretty. I like her swag." Scar answered.
"Noodles is a special gem in the hood. You know that's Trigga's little sister."
"Nah! I never knew that."
"She was raised with her mother in Japan and came to the states a few years back. You know Trigga be making sure she wants for nothing."
"That's what's up," Scar said, as he studied the interior of the BMW.
"I like this shit. How much you pay for this bad boy?"
"I paid sixty stacks." Streets answered.
"Damn, this is expensive."
"Yeah! It's a six series. This is just one of my toys. I have a navy blue Seven Series BMW and a pearl white Jaguar. Do you know how to

drive?"

"Nah!"

"If you want I'll teach you when you're ready."

"Alright dawg, we can do that."

"How long is your program?" Streets asked as he pulled up to the D.R.C. program.

"About an hour," Scar said, as he saw his man Murder across the street. *"Look at my nigga Murder getting that paper."* Scar said to himself.

"I will swing back through in an hour to pick you up," Streets said, as he gave Scar dap and walked inside the anger management program.

Chapter 6

Scar went inside the D.R.C. and headed straight to the anger management program. An hour later he finished the program, signed out and walked into the lobby. He saw his man Alex in the lobby and walked toward him. Scar and Alex formed a bond in Worcester Secure Treatment and been tight since.

"ALEX." Scar yelled as he reached him.
"SCAR. WHEN DID YOU GET HOME?"

Blammer was talking to his caseworker when he heard Alex shout Scar's name. He looked and saw Scar and Alex hugging like long lost brothers. He finished his conversation and walked out of the building. "I came home a couple of weeks back," Scar said, as he stared at his man Alex in the eyes.

"I thought you were committed to your twenty-first birthday?"

"I am. They let me go two months after my eighteenth birthday. What are you doing out here my nigga?" Scar asked as he stared at Alex's diamond chain.

"I'm doing a little something with my brother up in Archdale, but I think I'm about to jump on this heroin wave and get some real paper," Alex said, "I see you staring at my Atlanta Braves hat nigga. We rock those up in Archdale as well."

"I can see. Be careful wearing that hat. You don't want to get mistaken for one of us," Scar said.

"I'm good, I stay with the heat, plus we have Archdale stitched on the side of our hats. So, niggas don't get it mistaken. I like that t-shirt," Alex said, as he pointed to Scar's gang-affiliated T-shirt.

"You know I gotta rep the hood," Scar said with a smile on his face.

Scar finished talking to Alex and walked outside. As he walked down the steps, he heard someone call his name. He looked around and saw a dark skin youngster walking toward him with a Philadelphia Phillies Cap. *"He must be from Columbia Point."* Scar thought.

"Yo! Your name is Scar, from the A?" Blammer asked walking toward Scar.

"Yeah! What's up. Who you?" Scar asked.

"Blammer from the Point. I have been waiting to get with you for a while."

"About what?" Scar asked.

"My older brother," Blammer responded.

"Your older brother! Who's your older brother?" Scar asked as he stepped back a few feet.

"Faury," Blammer responded, looking Scar in the eyes.

"My cousin Faury? Scar asked.

"Yeah! The nigga you were locked up for killing," Blammer said, as he continued staring at Scar, "this is my first time meeting you and I always wanted to know what really happened and to hear your side of the story because everyone is saying something different."

Scar didn't like the tone in Blammer's voice, but he decided to give him his side of the story. Before Scar began to speak Murder walked up.

"What's up dawg," Murder said, as he gave Scar dap and looked at Blammer, "My name is Murder," he said, as he gave Blammer a pound.

"Blammer," Blammer responded.

"Where are you from?" Murder asked.

"The Point." Blammer answered as he looked at Scar, "so finish telling me what happened."

Scar felt Blammer was trying to press him and he didn't like that, "This is not the time nor the place. We will talk later." Scar said.

"Nah! We need to talk now. This is important. This is family shit." Blammer responded.

"I don't really know what y'all speaking about but this is my nigga."

Murder said pointing to Scar.

"This ain't got nothing to do with you, my man. This some personal family shit." Blammer said as he looked at Murder with death in his eyes.

Murder looked at Scar and asked. "Yo! Is this nigga your cousin?"

"That's my cousin's brother," Scar answered, as he turned to Blammer, "just go," Scar said, as he waved Blammer off.

"Okay Scar. If that's how you want it then that is how you going to get it," Blammer said, feeling disrespected how Scar had waived him off.

"Get what?" Scar asked, becoming angry.

"You know what it is. I came in peace. We could have talked this out." Blammer said.

"Hold up my man! Could have talked what out. Are you trying to send a threat?" Murder asked as he lifted his shirt showing his gun. He let the shirt drop back over the gun and stared at Blammer.

Blammer shook his head and turned to Scar, "I waited years to see you to have this talk and you want to flex on me in front of your man. I just asked you what happened that's all and your man wants to flash hammers.

"You know what. Fuck you." Murder said, "I can do whatever I want, how I want and when I want. If you don't like me flashing hammers, then get with me."

Blammer saw Alex standing on the stairs of the D.R.C. and saw his Atlanta Braves Cap and mistaken him as being from Academy Homes.

"*It's too many of these niggas,*" Blammer thought, "*I'm taking this one out on Scar,*" Blammer looked at Scar and said, "I'm out."

When Blammer walked away, Murder turned to Scar and said. "What that nigga wanted?"

"He asked me about some old shit." Scar answered.

"Check this out dawg, never let a nigga press you for anything you don't want to speak about. Tell a nigga to get on. You have to think like a man and not a scared boy. Be a dawg nigga in these streets and take no shit from no one."

"Alright."

"What you need some heat dawg. I got all types of guns if you need something speak up because niggas don't play fair." Murder said looking Scar in the eyes.

"I got heat," Scar said, as he thought about the gun under his bed.

"Use it when necessary, because any day could be your last like my man Ruthless Rick said 'bullets have no name, so squeeze before you get squeezed on.'"

Scar listened to the jewels that Murder was giving him and agreed with every word.

"Yo! Dawg. This D.R.C. shit is a trap for a nigga who isn't from around here. I be seeing all types of niggas up here. Be careful and stay strapped. Where are you going, back to your hood?" Murder asked as he saw people boarding the number 22 MBTA bus.

"Nah! My man Streets is coming to scoop me. Matter fact, let me call him," Scar said as he pulled out his phone and dialed Street's number and told him that he was finished. Ten minutes later Streets pulled up in his Six-Series BMW.

"That's my ride," Scar said, as he gave Murder dap and walked toward the BMW.

Chapter 7

Blammer couldn't believe how Scar had reacted. He walked down Centre Street and turned onto Wainwright Street and saw a group of niggas inside a basketball court.

"*I can't believe Scar let this nigga Murder interfere. Who the fuck this kid Murder anyways? Next time I see him I'm going to let my gun do the talking,*" Blammer said to himself, as he walked inside the park.

"BLAMMER!" Insane Dave yelled as he threw his hands in the air.

Blammer walked over to Insane Dave and gave him dap and a hug. He looked at the goons who surrounded Insane Dave and gave each one dap. "*These Wainright niggas look grimy.*" Blammer thought.

"What are you doing around here dawg?" Insane Dave asked.

"I just came from this D.R.C. shit and had some words with some niggas from Academy."

"Word. I never knew the Point had beef with the A?" Insane Dave asked.

"We don't. It's a long story on what went down dawg. I know I'm not letting this one go."

"What you need some heat dawg?" Insane Dave asked.

"Nah! I'm not going to crash and spray up the D.R.C. I'm just going to wait and get at them niggas next time we bump heads."

"I'm here all day in this park if I'm not here then I'll be over on Lithgow Street. So, if you need me just holler."

"Good looking out. Thanks for the offer. I was just seeing if you were out here before I hop on this train. I'm about to get out of here but I will def holler at you dawg," Blammer said, as he gave Insane Dave dap and walked toward Shawmut train station.

Blammer made it to the train station, pulled out his Charlie Card and scanned it. He stepped on the train platform and waited for the train. Ten minutes later he heard his train coming and stepped forward.

"Next time I see Scar and Murder, it's going to be more than words. Don't no one wave me off, flash hammers and don't shoot." Blammer said to himself.

* * * * * *

Scar sat in the passenger seat of Streets BMW listening to music. His thoughts were on what had transpired with Blammer. He always heard that his cousin Faury had a little brother but he had never met him until today. Streets pulled up inside a garage and parked. They stepped out and walked to the elevator. Scar saw a thick light skin female, walk past them.

"Excuse me, excuse me can I have a word with you?" Scar said, as he walked toward the female.

The light skin female stopped, looked at Scar as he walked toward her. *"Damn, he looks familiar,"* she thought, as she stared at Scar.

"Hey, how you doing? What's your name?" Scar asked.

"I'm doing fine, thanks for asking. My name is Mia. What's yours?"

"Shyheim, but everyone calls me Scar. I saw you walk by and I had to stop you to at least compliment you on your beauty."

"Well thanks, Shyheim, you don't look too bad yourself." Mia winked, "Have we met before? You look familiar."

"No! I don't think we ever crossed paths before."

"Are you sure?" Mia asked.

"Positive," Scar said, as he thought about all the years that he had spent in the Department of Youth Services. He saw that Mia was older and by the way she dressed showed that she had a little class. "What brings you to the mall today?"

"I'm on my way to work. I work over at the Coach store."

"Coach. Are there any benefits to working there? Do you get a discount or commission?" Streets chimed in.

"We get an employee discount and the pay is pretty fair. What about you where do you work?" Mia asked looking at Scar.

"I'm currently unemployed." Scar smiled.

"You look young. How old are you?"

"Eighteen." Scar answered.

"Oh! You're a baby. How old do you think I am?"

"Twenty-seven, Twenty-eight." Scar guessed.

"Thank you. But no. I'm a little older than that try mid-thirties."

"Damn, this bitch is old enough to be my moms," Scar thought, "you look good for your age," Scar complimented, "if it's not a problem can we exchange numbers."

"Sure," Mia said.

Scar pulled out his cell phone and passed it to Mia. She grabbed the phone, punched her number in and handed it back to Scar.

"Well, it was nice meeting you. I have to go to work. Make sure that you call me so we can talk more."

"I will." Scar answered as Mia started to walk away. He walked over to where Streets was at.

"I see you scored on that one my nigga."

"Yeah! She's a nice one dawg," Scar said, as they walked inside the mall.

Streets bought Scar a couple of outfits, sneakers, and some accessories. They stopped at the food court and ate some Burger King. "Thanks dawg, I appreciate all you did for a me today. I'm about to head home."

"You know how we roll dawg. Where do you live? You need me to drop you off? Where do you live?"

"I'm good. I live in Norwood. I can hop on the train at Back Bay."

"Oh alright, my Nigg, be safe and if you need me you got the number."

"I will be getting up." Scar said, as he gave Streets dap and walked away. As he rode down the escalator, he thought about what Murder said about the D.R.C. being a trap. He decided to no longer participate in the program or follow any of the Department of Youth Services rules. *"First thing in the morning, I'm hopping on the plane and going to visit my dad."*

Chapter 8

The plane landed at Phoenix Sky Harbor International Airport. Scar reached in the overhead and grabbed a small bag that had his toiletries, underclothes and his phone charger.

He stepped off the plane and walked through the gate, down to the escalator onto the baggage claim and out of the doors to the taxi stand.

Uncle Stretch stood outside of the airport in a two-piece linen suit and some Gucci driving shoes. His eyes were shielded by a pair of gold rimmed Gucci Sunglasses. He saw his son walk out of the airport, lifted his sunglasses to his forehead, called his son's name and waved his arms. "SHYHEIM."

Scar heard his father's voice shout his name. He looked and saw his father thirty feet away waving his arms trying to get his attention. Scar walked toward his father, "What's up pops," Scar said, as he hugged his father.

"Welcome to Arizona son. I'm glad that you made it." Uncle Stretch said, as he grabbed Scar's bag.

"It looks like Arizona is treating you good," Scar said playfully punching his father in the chest.

"Good, is an understatement. Arizona is treating me great." Uncle Stretch said, as he steered toward his car, "you going to love it out here everything is beautiful from the weather to the scenery and the women make the scenery that much better."

"Where's Broad Jay?"

"In Nevada. He's out there holding that side of the business down," Uncle Stretch said as he walked to a navy-blue Audi R-8.

Scar followed his father to the car, "Wow! Dad, Arizona is treating you great! What kind of car is this pop?" Scar asked, as he walked around the car slowly. He stopped at the rear of the car and looked at the transparent hooded engine.

"Damn, niggas weren't lying when they said my pops was the man,"

Scar thought, "Damn, pops, that's the engine."

"Yeah!"

"I like this. This is one hell of a car," Scar said, as he slid in the passenger seat.

Uncle Stretch put Scar's bag in the trunk and then joined his son in the car.

"Dad, why is the engine in the back?" Scar asked.

"Because the engine comes in the back in most exotic sports car of this caliber."

"Oh! I never knew that."

"It's called living in exclusivity." Uncle Stretch laughed, "How are you transitioning back home?"

"Good. I'm still trying to figure out a few things," Scar said, as he played with the levers, knobs and switches trying to find the radio.

"Hold up. This is how you do it," Uncle Stretch said, as he showed his son how to pull the Pandora app up, "what you want to hear?"

"Chief Keef."

After Uncle Stretch pressed the command for voice activation, he told Scar to speak what he wanted to hear.

"CHIEF KEEF." Scar shouted.

"You don't have to shout it," Uncle Stretch laughed, "you can fill me in on everything you been going through when we get to the house.

"Okay." Scar said.

Uncle Stretch pulled out of the airport and hit the Pierswa Freeway and drove North. He turned onto the Pima Highway and then drove East to Scottsdale.

Scar relaxed as he watched miles and miles of desert flash by while Chief Keef flowed through the custom surround sound system.

"Wow! Arizona is really the desert," Scar said, as he stared at the desert landscape.

 Twenty minutes later Uncle Stretch pulled into a paved driveway of a 6,000 square foot Santa-Barbara style house that sat on two acres of land in North Scottsdale. He parked next to his Westminster Edition Range Rover and a black 7 Series BMW.

"Damn, my dad is really the man." Scar thought, as he stepped out and walked to the trunk. He grabbed his bag and followed his father up the stone entryway into the house. The first thing Scar took in was the foyer, to the left of the foyer was the living room. The living room had a chaise, sofa, end tables, chairs and oil paintings hung on the wall. Scar didn't know nothing about art, but he figured the oil paintings were worth a lot of money. He placed down his bags on the chaise and then followed his father through an 18-foot floor to ceiling electronic glass door that led to an outdoor covered patio. Uncle Stretch sat down in the outside area on the patio that overlooked the

mountains. "Dad, this house is nice how much did you pay for this? The view is something else. I never seen anything like this, especially in Boston." Scar said, as he stared at the mountain views.

"This house and the acres of land cost me about seven hundred thousand. It was one of my best investments that I ever made. Arizona has treated me well, since I came out here, I was able to flip a few commercial and residential properties and create a nice flow of income. I used the money that I earned from the real estate game to clean up the money I made in Boston. Let me show you the house and the basement.

The basement is something special. I want nothing more than to have you out here living with me."

"I want to come too, but my caseworker won't approve of me coming to live here. So, I have to wait till I am twenty-one years old."

"How is your transition back into the world?"

"It's coming along, dad, I want to tell you something. I don't know where to begin."

"The beginning. The problems I have are minimal, but they have the potential to get out of hand." Scar said, as he looked at his father in the eyes. "It's this one nigga from the hood that I might have to murder one day."

"What do you mean by that. The A is our home it's love there. What people isn't respecting the reputation I carved there?"

"It's not that. When I first came home and was introduced to everyone it was love but the older head Free resented me for the problems he had with you. Every chance he got he tried to punk me and it irritated him that I wasn't taking no shorts or scared of him. He was talking shit about you running to the West Coast because you're scared and some other shit, I didn't pay no attention to.

"He said that?" Uncle Stretch asked.

"Yeah."

"Why you never told me about this when it happened?"

"Dad, I didn't want to pull you into this. I can handle him and his crew. While me and Free was going through our problems I ran into a nigga from the Point name Blammer. He stepped to me outside of this anger management program asking me about what happened to his brother."

"His brother! Who is his brother?"

"My cousin Faury."

"Who are you talking about Nastees' son "Byron?" Uncle Stretch said, as he thought about how Nastee hated the gangsters that claimed Academy Homes.

"Yes." Scar replied, "well we had words and my man Murder flashed a gun and didn't use it."

"That's a no-no. You never flash a gun and don't use it. That might have been a mistake if Byron is about his business he might try to get at your man, whatever you do next time you see Byron, tell him what happened and put that shit to rest."

"I will."

"Well, relax son we are going to have a good time out here. I'm going to take you out to get something to eat and then I want you to get some rest and clear your head because I know it was a long flight."

"Sounds like a plan.

Chapter 9

Scar woke up the next morning and the first thing he did was grab his toiletry bag and walked to the bathroom. He opened the bag, pulled out his toothbrush and applied some toothpaste and started brushing his teeth. After he finished brushing his teeth, he took a quick shower and stepped out and walked to the closet. He opened the door and saw that it was filled with linen and cotton suits. He picked through the linen suits and pulled out a sky-blue suit, white cream shirt and walked over to the bed and placed it down.

"Yeah! This can work," Scar said, as he stared at the suit. He grabbed his house coat and some Adidas slides and left the room. He walked down the spiral stairs that led to the main floor of the house and into the dining room. He saw his father in the dining room reading a newspaper.

"Good morning dad."

"Good morning son."

"What are you reading?"

"The Wall Street Journal. Are you hungry?"

"Am I? I'm starving."

"Good. Maritza is preparing breakfast for us."

"Who's Maritza?" Scar asked.

"Maritza's my personal chef. Do you like Spanish omelets?"

"Yeah!" Scar said, as he thought about the Spanish omelets that his mother used to make when he was a child.

Ten minutes later an older Hispanic female stepped in the dining room with two plates of home fries, eggs, turkey sausage and raisin bagels in her hands. She placed the plates in front of Scar and his father.

"Maritza, this is my son Shyheim."

"Hola, Shyheim," Maritza greeted in her Spanish accent. "It's nice to meet you."

"Nice to meet you too. Damn, dad you got maids, personal chefs and I wouldn't be surprised if you had a butler."

"I do." Uncle Stretch said seriously. "So, let's talk about your future and your plans now that you are out of that situation. So, what is it that you want to do with your life?"

"I was thinking about enrolling in school and taking up a business course or something."

"What kind of business course? Because they have a few classes that you can take and what about location, do you know which school you want to go to or do you want to take the community college route?"

"I think I'm going to roll with the community college for now and once I get situated then I will enroll in a university. Never know I might be going to school out here."

"I would love that. I been dealing with Real estate since I been down here and have a nice little portfolio. When the time is right, I will give you the game on that so that you can add on to my business."

"Okay." Scar said.

Then the doorbell ring. He watched as an older brown skin man with salt and pepper hair step out of the den and walk to the door. *"Damn, that must be the butler."* Scar thought. He saw the butler walk back in the living room with a man with a clean shaved head and salt and pepper beard.

Broad Day Jay saw Uncle Stretch and Scar sitting at the dining table eating breakfast. He saw how big Scar had gotten and cracked a smile. Scar saw that the man walking toward them was Broad Day Jay.

"Jay, what's up?" Scar said, as he hugged the man who taught him how to shoot a gun.

"Damn, boy look at you all tall and shit. Last time I saw you was when you were a little nigga. Look at you with that little peach fuzz on your chin." Broad Day Jay said referring to the strings of hair on Scar's chin, "How was your trip?"

"It was a good trip, but long. I had gotten some much needed rest last night."

"Well, you here with us, what's up bro." Broad Day Jay said, as he hugged Uncle Stretch. "Man, y'all look like twins."

"What you mean look like twins, he is my twin," Uncle Stretch joked. Soon as we finished eating, we going to take him out and show him how we are living out here in the west."

The next six hours Uncle Stretch and Broad Day Jay showed Scar everything there was in the Scottsdale and Phoenix areas of Arizona. Scar couldn't believe how pretty the females were and knew that once he had gotten from the grips of the Department of Youth Services that he would be joining his father and godfather.

Chapter 10

Scar spent three days in Arizona and then flew back to Boston. He was still in awe about how his father was living out west. The first thing he had done once he went back home was talk to his mother about furthering his education. He kissed his mother and left the house and decided to take another route to the city. He walked to the bus stop and waited for the city bus.

Fifteen minutes later the bus pulled up and Scar stepped on. He found a seat in the back and sat down. He went into deep thought about what Murder had told him. *"You need money to win a war."* Those words were all that was being replayed in his head repeatedly. Scar knew to go against Blammer, Monster, Free and any others who deemed him an enemy would be an obstacle that he needed money for. Scar stepped off the bus at Forest Hills Bus and Train Station and took another bus. He was so deep in thought that he missed his stop.

"Oh shit!" Scar said as he pressed the ringer.

The bus stopped outside of the St. Joseph Housing Development. He stepped off the bus and saw Riot's Mercedes Benz parked inside of the St. Joseph Housing Development. He cut across the lot, into the project and saw Riot's Atlanta Braves cap turned backwards talking to a few people. One of the niggas talking to Riot pointed in the direction of Scar. Riot turned around and threw his hands up from the window of the store, Scar watched dope fiends walking around aimlessly in search of their next fix. He wondered why the addicts walked around empty-handed.

"Damn, all these dope fiends and no dope," a nigga named Hawk said.
"Is this a dope block?" Scar asked.
"Was a dope block. This was one of the top dope blocks in the city, but shit been dry since L.L., Deek, and Munch disappeared. Since then niggas been selling crack," Hawk said showing Scar a mouth full of twenty rocks.

Scar pulled Riot to the side and asked him to speak to a few elders from St. Joe about niggas opening a shop in the projects. Riot looked at Scar like he was crazy and called an older head named Slice over. Slice walked over and listened to what Riot asked. He looked at Scar and then gave the clearance but with stipulations that he only could hustle across from the project on a street called Regent. Scar dapped Riot and the rest of the crew and cut through Washington Park and flagged down a taxi. He opened the door and directed the driver to Codman Square. He had to pay Murder a visit.

* * * * * *

Murder was handling business on his block when he saw a red and white taxi drive by. He looked at the taxi and saw a nigga staring at him. Murder threw his hands in the air, enticing the passenger. The taxi stopped and Murder reached in his waist. He looked closely and saw Scar's Atlanta Braves cap. Scar stepped out, walked over, and hugged Murder. They walked down the street and into one of Murder's dope houses.

"What's good?" Murder said.

"I came to holler at you about an important issue." Scar said.

"Is everything alright? What's up?" Murder asked.

"I need some work."

"Now you getting money? What you at war?" Murder asked as he studied the expression on Scar's face.

"Yeah and No! I want to get my money right so I can take it to these bitch ass Heath Street and Orchard Park niggas. Especially, Monster's bitch ass."

"Monster. That nigga goes hard but if you going to bring it to him then bring it hard because he plays no games and plays with no rules." Murder said seriously, as he pulled out three bundles of heroin and passed it to Scar. "Do you know what that is?"

"What?" Scar asked.

"That's three bundles. I'm going to show you the ropes of this dope game, it isn't all about selling it, you need to know everything from shaking it, packaging it and telling good dope from bad dope," Murder said, as he pulled out a wax bag from his sleeve and cracked it open.

Scar watched as Murder poured two lines on the table and snorted one. He lifted his head and pointed to Scar.

"I'm good," Scar said with his hands raised in surrender mode.

"Ya good, how I'm going to teach you about this shit dawg if you don't sniff this shit? How you going to tell good dope from bad dope? Don't be a little bitch ass nigga! Sniff that shit!" Murder demanded.

"I'm far from a bitch ass nigga," Scar responded, feeling violated that Murder called him a bitch ass nigga.

"Well you are acting like a scary bitch ass nigga!" Murder said, eyeing Scar down.

Scar hesitated and then followed what he saw Murder do. He didn't want to make Murder mad and fuck an opportunity to get real money. He lowered his head and snorted the heroin. Scar lifted his head and experienced a high that he would never forget. He placed the bundles in his pocket.

"That's good dope," Murder said.

They walked out of the house and Murder flagged down a taxi. Scar looked at him and asked.

"What do I owe you?"

"Nothing. You are my man. This one's on me, but next time I will charge you sixty dollars for every gram.

Scar stepped inside of the taxi and sat in the back seat high as hell. He couldn't believe that heroin had him feeling like he was on cloud nine. He pulled up to St. Joe's, stepped out, and walked up to Slice and pulled out the bundles. "Let's get money." Scar said.

Chapter 11

"A trader made an inter-orientation that they would receive more gold for their labor." Scar thought as he listened to Slice expound on the money coming in and out of St. Joseph and how he needed Scar's presence to be the money tree. *"This nigga think my labor is going to make him rich. He got another thing coming if he is going to sit up at home and wait for me to bring him food."* Scar thought. "They don't call me Asiatic for nothing." Scar thought as he reflected on how deep the lessons of the Nation of Gods & Earths were.

The next hour Scar and Slice discussed how they would operate the business in the St. Joseph Housing Development. Scar liked the idea of getting money in St. Joe's and knew if the Department of Youth

Services were to look for him the first place they would look is at his house and then the Academy Homes. He stashed the heroin in a hallway on Regent Street and told Slice he would be back and left. He walked to the Academy Homes, saw Pitt and a few others outside of Kia's apartment building and walked toward them. He gave dap to everyone and pulled Pitt to the side. He told Pitt about his status with the Department of Youth Services and asked if it was okay if he can lay low at Kia's apartment. Pitt gave him the green light, but Scar still wanted to ask Kia to make sure everything was cool. Scar walked inside Kia's apartment and saw her sitting in the living room watching the movie "South Central".

"I see you watching my favorite movie," Scar said, as he slid on the couch next to Kia.

"What's up Scar? I'm trying to see why you like this movie so much," Kia said playfully.

"I like it so much because it's a classic. Sis, I need to talk to you."

"Is everything alright?" Kia asked concerned.

"Yeah! Everything is cool. Do you remember when you said that your house is my home?"

"Yup, and I mean it," Kia answered.

"Well, I need to lie low here for the next few weeks. I kept running into problems at the D.R.C. and decided to go AWOL from these programs that my caseworker is making me do. Any day now she's going to put out a warrant and I just want to be two steps ahead."

"I told you when I first met you that my house is your home. You can either sleep in the living room or my son's room. Whichever is convenient for you."

"Well, I don't want my presence to be any inconvenience."

"Never that. You are family."

"That's good to know. I'm only going to be here for a few weeks until I'm able to stack some money and get my own spot."

"Scar, you can stay as long as you need to."

"Alright. Thanks sis," Scar said, as he gave Kia a hug. He walked out of Kia's apartment and joined Pitt and the rest of the crew outside. He was still feeling high from the heroin that he had sniffed earlier. *"Damn, this dog food got me high as hell,"* Scar thought,

"Yo Pitt, did the D-boys come through here today?"

"Yeah! They were around earlier harassing niggas." Pitt answered.

"I have to be on the low because if I get caught sleeping then I'm back to juvenile detention for the next three years." Scar said.

"Just move on the low out here and play the back streets" Pitt said.

"Yeah! I know. I found a spot to get money at." Scar said.

"Where at?" Pitt asked.

"St. Joe's." Scar answered.

"The Joes. There's a little money down there. Who you know down there?"

"A few niggas," Scar said, as he thought about the agreement he had made with Slice. "I'm about to bounce. I'll see y'all later," Scar said, as he gave his crew dap.

Chapter 12

Scar finished the heroin that Murder had given him the next day. He and Slice assured the dope fiends that there would be a constant supply of heroin in the project. He sniffed a few bags of heroin with Slice and was starting to become addicted. It was time for him to re-up. He flagged down a taxi and went to Codman Square to holler at Murder.

Scar met Murder at the same dope house. Murder immediately noticed little changes and questioned Scar about his heroin use. Scar admitted that he and the older head Slice had been sniffing together.

"Nigga you can't let that shit control you. You must control that. Look at you, clothes all wrinkled and shit. Police look for niggas like that.

Clean that up. Matter fact come on," Murder said. They walked down Washington Street to a store named "Northside". "How much money you have?" Murder asked.

"A few hundred."

"That's enough. Let me get three black Champion hoodies," Murder said, as he looked at Scar and shook his head.

Scar didn't understand Murder's reasons for buying him the hoodies in the summertime. "What you need hoodies for in this weather?" Scar asked.

"Nigga, hoodies are for all year round. These are the most needed out of anything in the hood. These shits aren't for me these are yours." Murder said.

Murder paid for the hoodies and passed the bag to Scar, "clean that shit up and control that shit nigga." Scar nodded his head and knew he was falling off. They walked back to the dope house and Scar reached in his pocket and grabbed his money. He passed the bills to Murder. Murder counted the money, left the room and came back with a brick of heroin.

"Get money nigga. This is five hundred bags in these streets this is known as a brick." Murder said passing Scar the brick.

Scar looked at the brick and then at Murder and said, "you never lied."

"There's no reason. All I know is to get money, fuck bitches and lay heads to rest."

"I hear that." Scar agreed.

"What you better do is shake that shit you let control you. Fuck around, nigga be nodding somewhere and get your shit pushed back in the streets."

Scar listened to the wisdom Murder gave him agreed and decided to lower his usage of heroin and focus on getting money. He saw a taxi at a stoplight and waved his hand in the air. The taxi pulled over. Scar gave Murder dap and slid in the back seat and directed the driver to St. Joes. The taxi pulled up to Regent Street and the first thing Scar saw was Riot's Mercedes Benz parked. He stepped out of the taxi and walked into an alley to stash the brick. He walked out of the alley and over toward where Riot stood.

"What's up dawg?" Scar said, as he gave Riot a hug.
"Getting this money. I see why niggas say there's no money like dope money. I saw so many dope fiends around here today it made me want to switch from the coke game to the dope game," Riot joked. "Be careful out here dawg. The dope game brings a lot of police pressure, my nigga, you also need to watch out for these dope fiends they act crazy at times."
"I know. I had to threaten a few already. What are you doing out here?"
"I had to holler at a few niggas before I go and pick up my girl. What are you doing?"
"Getting right." Scar said, "why, what's up?"
"Take a ride with me to pick my girl up. She has this freaky ass friend that likes young gangsters."
"Word." Scar said.
"Yeah! She's a little older, but she is pretty and doesn't look her age."

"Let me slide Slice some of these bundles before I bounce," Scar said, as he walked away.

Riot walked to his car and waited for Scar. A few minutes later Scar walked over and got in the passenger seat. Riot pulled off and drove toward Tremont Street.

"Where does she live?" Scar asked.

"Allston." Riot answered.

Scar watched the bus routes and street signs on Tremont Street. He studied each food franchise that they had passed. This was his way of learning the city.

Riot pulled into a parking lot of a string of condominiums and parked. Scar stepped out and walked to a set of stairs and leaned against the railing. Riot stepped out and walked up the steps. As they approached the door it swung open.

"Hola," Riot's girl Tessie greeted.

"Hey, baby," Riot said, as he hugged and kissed her. "This is my man Scar."

"Hi Scar," Tessie said, as she gave Scar a hug.

They walked inside the apartment and into the kitchen. Scar smelled the aroma of his favorite food, chicken.

"It smells good in here," Riot said, as he spotted Mia at the stove, "what's up Mia."

"What's up Riot," Mia said as she emptied a skillet of chicken strips onto some paper towels.

Scar watched Mia empty the chicken strips and smiled. He noticed that Mia was the same female he had met at the mall with Streets. He stared at her thick hips and round butt.

Mia placed a handful of chicken strips in the skillet and turned to Scar. She was taken back at his appearance. The wrinkle shirt and jeans had him looking like a street bum. She looked closer and saw it was the same person she met at the mall.

"Hi, Shyheim," Mia said.

"You two know each other?" Riot asked.

"Yeah! We met before," Scar answered.

"Shyheim's a cute name. I like that," Mia said.

"Whatever happened to you calling me back?" Mia asked.

"The phone number I gave you was a throwaway phone and some shit happened and I had to toss it." Scar lied.

"Yeah! Okay," Mia said sarcastically. "Are you hungry?" Mia asked.

"Yeah! What you putting together?" Scar asked.

"Chicken strips and fries," Mia said, as she eyed Scar's fuzzy braids, "you should let me braid your hair."

"We could arrange that." Scar smiled.

"You have long hair," Tessie said, "How long have you been growing your hair?"

"Since I was ten years old."

"Ten! How old are you now?" Tessie asked.

"Eighteen."

"Wow, you been growing your hair for eight years," Tessie said, as she fixed Riot a plate.

"Do you know how old Mia is?"

"Yeah! She is in her mid-thirties." Scar answered. "I like older women they are more experienced."

"I like younger men they are more energetic," Mia said, as she licked her lips.

"Mia, stop being nasty," Tessie said, as she placed a plate in front of Riot and Scar.

Scar started to eat the food without blessing it. Mia looked at him like he was a lunatic.

"Damn, nigga! Say a prayer to God." Mia said.

"Fuck God! I am God!" Scar answered.

Mia looked at Scar, his unibrow, and wanted him badly. She knew that she had seen him before, but didn't know from where.

"I didn't mean to disrespect your lord, my father's part of the Nation of Gods and Earth and the lessons I study teach me that I'm God."

"Sounds like a cult," Mia said.

"Never. It's a Nation of righteous men and women who teach the proper form of Islam which is peace." Mia listened to him and was beginning to like his style.

"That's okay. I don't know too much about the Nation of Gods and Earths except that the Wu-Tang Clan and Rakim were members. Maybe one day you can teach me more about it."

"Anytime let me know when," Scar said, as he looked Mia in the eyes.

"What are you doing for the fourth of July?" Mia asked

"I'll be at Academy Day." Scar answered.

"Oh! Alright! I was going to ask if you wanted to watch the fireworks at the Esplanade with me."

"Maybe next year. This is my first Academy Day and I can't miss it for nothing."

"I understand," Mia said.

"Where's the bathroom at?"

"Down the hall to the left," Mia answered.

Scar excused himself and walked toward the bathroom. He mistakenly walked inside of Mia's bedroom. He stopped at the door and admired the lay-out on how she had the walls painted a peach hue, a California king size bed with a white leather headboard, wall to wall peach carpet and mirrors that lined the walls and ceilings. He stared at a giant flat screen that was mounted on the wall between two mirrors. He turned around and saw a bathroom and stepped inside. He used the toilet, washed his hands and walked out.

Mia was in the kitchen cleaning when he walked past, "alright Scar, it was nice seeing you again. You know the address don't be a stranger, nigga," Mia said with a grin on her face, "matter fact, here, take my number, she wrote it down on a piece of paper and passed it to Scar. Scar grabbed the piece of paper and stepped out of the condominium. He opened the car door and slid in the rear seat. Riot dropped Tessie off in a housing project called Villa Victoria in the south end of the city.

"What you think I should name my son? I'm going to name all my kids after guns. Tessie wants to name him after a Cuban hero named "Che."

"What about Ruger," Scar offered.

"Yeah! I thought about that, but I'm leaning more towards Taurus."

A black Seven Series BMW pulled beside them. Scar saw the BMW and reached for his waist and asked.

"Who's that?"

"That's my nigga Streets from Castlegate," Riot said, as he rolled down the passenger window.

"Oh! That's my nigga," Scar said, as he put the gun down and stuck his head out the window and told Streets to pull over.

Streets pulled over and stepped out. He walked to the sidewalk and waited for them to join him. Scar stepped out and joined Streets on the sidewalk.

"What's up my nigga?" Scar asked, as he gave Streets dap.

"Just living within my means," Streets answered.

"I see," Scar said, as he eyed the twenty-two-inch Lexani rims on the BMW.

Riot walked over and gave Streets dap, "What's up my nigga?"

"Living. What you'll doing tonight?" Streets asked.

"Nothing. Why, what's good?" Riot answered.

"I'm throwing a sleazy skate-off at Che-Vous, come and show some love."

"We will be there dawg. What's up with my cousin Raw Raw?" Scar asked.

"He's chilling. I just spoke to him earlier. I told him that we got up and he told me to tell you to keep your head up and he will see you when he comes home."

"Alright. Let him know that the family misses him and can't wait for him to be back amongst us." Scar said.

"Will do. I'll see you tonight." Streets said, as he got back in his car and pulled off.

Scar and Riot hopped back in the car and drove off. Scar knew he had to get his paper game up so he could be driving whatever he chose but first he had to kick the heroin habit he now had.

Chapter 13

Che-Vous was a local skating rink behind Mattapan's area police precinct. The skating rink was a deadly place in the city over the last three decades.

This was the place where some of the worst gangsters in the city earned their reputation.

Scar sat in the passenger seat of Riot's Mercedes-Benz looking at all the females in skimpy outfits. Riot found a parking spot and parked. Scar stepped out and walked down the street. He found a stash spot and pulled out his .380 Revolver and stashed it in a Doritos Bag behind a fence. After he stashed the gun, he walked up the street and joined his crew. They walked inside the skating rink and the first-person Scar saw standing next to the pool tables was Blammer and a few members of his Columbia Point gang. Streets saw Scar, Riot and a few other members of Academies walk in and walked over to them and greeted each one with the three-finger handshake.

"I'm glad to see that y'all came out to support me today," Streets said. "It's all love dog," Scar said, as he saw a light skin female skating backward and waved at her.

Scar spoke a few minutes longer to Streets and slipped off into the bathroom. He opened a stall, walked in and pulled out a wax paper bag from his sleeve. He opened it and snorted two lines with each nose and then flushed the bag into the toilet. He walked to the sink and made sure no evidence was on his nose. He walked back and blended in with his crew. The thick light skin female that Scar waved at earlier rolled up on skates and sparked a conversation with him. Scar asked for her name and learned that it was Disney and that she was from Wildwood Street but lived with her grandmother on Lucerne Street. They exchanged numbers before she skated off.

Disney had stringy brownish hair that reached her neck, a bubble butt and a nice set of breasts. He watched her ass cheeks as she skated off. *"That was easy,"* Scar thought, as he saw Blammer and a few members of his gang walking toward him.

"Scar can I talk to you?" Blamer asked.

"Yeah what's up? Let's step over here," Scar said, as he walked a few feet away from his crew. "What do you want to talk about?" Scar asked.

"What I was trying to ask you that day at The Anger Management Program was what happened with my older brother because people keep saying to us that it was done on purpose."

"Nah! I would never kill him on purpose that was my cousin and best friend. Who told you that?"

"People who are supposed to be close to your family, but I don't know them to ask. So, I figured your free I'll try to holler at you and see what went down."

"Well. It was an accident. We were playing and the gun went off. We did not know that it was loaded."

"Alright thanks, dog, that's all I wanted to know," Blammer said giving Scar the three-finger handshake, "I see it's a lot of Braves hats here, where's your man? who was talking shit" Blammer said, looking for Murder.

"Who Murder? He's not from my Hood."

"He's not, where is he from?" Blammer asked.

"Codman Square. Why? What you trying to see him, or something, cause if you are trying to see him, I'm not feeling that. That's my man. I'm not with that." Scar said.

"What you mean? He pulled a gun out on me and didn't use it."

"Nah! Dog, that was just a misunderstanding he thought it was beef and he had my back and I got his. You need to let that go that's a misunderstanding."

"Alright. Since you said it like that then I am going to let that go,"

Blammer said, as he dapped Scar and walked away.

Scar walked over toward his crew and enjoyed the rest of the night. Fifteen minutes before midnight he slipped out and walk down the street. He reached behind the fence, grabbed the Dorito bag and pulled out his gun. He stashed it in his waist and waited for his crew to step out of the skating rink. He saw Disney step out of the skating rink and called her over. They spoke for a few minutes and she agreed to spend the night with him. She got in the backseat of the Mercedes. Disney set in the backseat quietly as Riot drove to a Mobile Gas Station in Egleston Square. On the ride to the Mobil Gas Station, Scar called his man Pitt. About time they pulled up Pitt was coming down the street on a mountain bike. He saw Scar, Riot, and Disney and hopped off the bike and saluted his crew with the three-finger handshake. Scar introduced Disney to Pitt.

"You smoke?" Pitt asked.
"Yeah!" Disney answered.
"Let's get out of here and go up in these woods and blow this weed" Pitt said as he rode the bike to the project.

Scott and Disney followed him up the hill toward the project and cut through the woods. Pitt Placed the bike near a tree, grabbed a blunt from behind his ear and lit It Up. Disney and Pitt shared the blunt while Scar stared into the empty project courtyard. He started to nod. Disney saw him nodding and asked. "Are you tired?" Scar opened his eyes and shook his head no.

"It's dark over there what happened to the street lights?" Disney asked.

"We shot them out so if the police come through here, they can't spot us," Pitt answered.

Is this the dark side or the light side? Disney asked

"Neither. This is the Four Squares. The Light Side is over there?" Pitt pointed to the right side "and the Dark Side is over there to the right. We are in the middle of the project." as he finished the last of the blunt. "Come on, let's go to Kia's," he said as he led the way out of the woods toward the Dark Side.

Pitt opened the door and pointed to Kia's son's room. Scar opened the door and Disney stepped into the room. She was in awe of all the Atlanta Braves memorabilia that Kia's son had. Scar took off his shirt placed it on the doorknob and walked to the bathroom. He saw the door was open, stepped in and locked it. He cut on the water, pulled out a bag from his sleeve, cracked the seal and snorted the contents. He washed his face, brushed his teeth, grabbed a warm rag and went back to the room to give Disney some dope dick.

Disney wanted to surprise Scar so she took off her sneakers, socks, jeans and her t-shirt. As she was unfastening her bra the door opened and Scar stepped into the room, he saw that she was practically naked and couldn't believe how pretty her bouncy breasts were. He looked at her breast, flat stomach and the lump between her thighs and knew this would be a night that she won't forget. He pulled out the .380 from his pocket, turned around and placed it on the dresser. He turned back around and saw that Disney's boy shorts were on the floor. Scar wasted no time taking off his sneaker's, jeans and boxers. He reached in his jeans and pulled out a condom and ripped it open with his teeth and rolled it onto his dick. He climbed onto the bed and pulled her close to him. As he entered her, she squirmed, moaned and scratched his back. He started pumping fast like a jackhammer. Disney screamed his name as he dug deeper and deeper inside her pussy. He flipped her over and started pounding her from the back with force. He pulled his dick out and laid on his back. She climbed on top of him, turned around and started riding him reverse cowgirl. He watched her ass cheeks clap on his dick like thunder. With his left hand, he slapped her red ass cheeks hard. He slapped each cheek four times before he saw a creamy liquid cover the condom. As she started to cum, she began to ride faster and harder. After two hours of sex, he felt his nut rising out the shaft of his dick and closed his eyes as the cum came out of the tip of his dick. She felt his liquid squirt in the condom and collapsed on his chest. He lifted her off him and saw the condom was ripped wide open.

"Damn." Scar thought.

Scar pushed her on the bed, got up, cleaned his dick with a warm Rag and sat on the edge of the bed. He heard Disney snoring and knew that he had just put that dope dick on her. He covered her naked body with a sheet, got up, grabbed his gun and walked into the living room to watch his favorite movie South Central.

Chapter 14

Disney woke up hours later and reached for scar. She noticed his side of the bed was empty. She sat up and saw a Walgreens bag on the nightstand. She opened the bag and noticed it was full of feminine hygiene products. She grabbed the bag and walked into the hallway in search of a bathroom. Her nostrils were filled with the fresh smell of breakfast. She walked past the living room and saw Scar sitting on the couch watching the movie South Central.

"He thinks he's OG Bobby Johnson," Kia said.

Disney Flinched as she saw Kia coming out of the kitchen with an oversized Atlanta Braves T-shirt with a gigantic A on the front.

"My name is Kia," Kia said, as she reached out her hand.

"My name is Disney. Nice to meet you, Kia. It smells good in here what are you cooking?" Disney asked as she shook Kia's hand.

"Where are you from?" Kia asked.

"The L," Disney said making an L sign with her fingers.

"Lenox Street Project?" Kia asked.

"Nah! Lucerne Street," Disney said feeling upset that Kia associated the L with Lenox Street.

"Oh! I thought the L stood for Lenox Street Project but make yourself at home. There are towels and face rags in the bathroom. I'm cooking breakfast so when you finish cleaning yourself your food will be done. Do you eat turkey bacon?"

"I never knew turkey made bacon," Disney bashfully said.

"Are you coming to family day?"

"I never knew I was invited," Disney said as she cut her eye at Scar.

"Scar didn't invite you?"

"No. When is it?"

"Tomorrow."

"Oh! No. I already made plans for the fourth with my family," Disney lied. "let me get in the shower," Disney said, as she turned and walked inside the bathroom. Disney took a quick shower and joined Scar in the living room. He was busy watching OG Bobby Johnson kill the Kansas City smack man. He felt Disney's tongue licking his ear lobe.

Kia came out of the kitchen and saw Disney sucking on Scar's ear. She placed the plate on the coffee table and giggled. Disney stopped giving Scar ear fellatio and picked up a piece of turkey bacon and bit into it. She looked at Kia and gave her a thumbs up. She finished her meal and called a taxi. Scar walked with Disney out front to wait for the taxi. Disney saw dozens of men young and old hustling selling drugs and playing dice. She looked at all the Atlanta Braves hats scattered around in the courtyard and started to do a silent count. She stopped at twenty-eight and said, *"damn these niggas are deep."*

A Red and White Taxi pulled up to Kia's apartment. Disney stepped off the stoop, kissed Scar on the cheek and walked toward the taxi switching hard. She opened the door, blew Scar an air kiss and slid in. Scar walked up to the driver and handed him a twenty-dollar bill, turned and walked over toward his crew. The taxi pulled off and stopped at a stoplight down the hill. Disney saw a few more niggas wearing Atlanta Braves Caps and then she knew that Academy was one of the deepest hoods in the city. The whole ride Disney thought about Scar, his big dick, her swollen pussy, and a possible future with him. All thoughts ceased as the taxi turned on Lucerne Street and she saw her man and his friends outside of her house.

Clapper stood on the stairs with a red and white St. Louis Cardinals Baseball Cap. He had a dog leash in his hand and an ice grill on his face. The taxi stopped and Disney watched Clapper walk down the stairs, swinging the dog leash in the air. She felt her stomach turn as she saw the homicidal look in his eyes. She wanted to tell the driver to keep driving but Clapper's right-hand man, "Kill at Will" was already at the door quizzing the driver. Disney opened the door and stepped out. Clapper grabbed a fist full of hair and pulled her close. He dropped the leash and slapped her. The force of his heavy hands crumpled her body to the pavement.

"Where you been at bitch?" Clapper asked, "My friend Lisha's crib." Disney lied. "She's lying. The driver said that he had picked her up down Academy," Kill at Will said.

"Academy. So, you're an Academy whore now? I never knew Lisha live in Academy." he yelled.

Clapper spit in her face and kicked her with his ragged construction Timberland Boots. She curled up in a fetal position and took the beating of her life. He punched, stomped and beat her with the dog leash. "The next time you disrespect me the penalty will be a bullet in your neck!" He growled.

Chapter 15

Scar watched Disney's taxi disappear and walked over to where his crew was posted at.

"That thick thing, was you?" Little Barry asked.

"Yeah, I met her last night at the Vous. It was a lot of pretty bitches up there. I never knew the Vous be poppin like that. That was my first time there." Scar said.

It's always popping on Friday Nights, but it's bad timing because it's either get that Friday night money or go there and get some pussy. With me, it's always money over bitches." Pitt said.

"That's why that early-morning heroin money is the best," Scar thought. "I am about to bounce I will see y'all niggas later. He said,

as he walked to Columbus Avenue and flagged a taxi.

The taxi stopped and Scar slid in the back seat. He directed the driver to Codman Square. As he sat in the back seat, he thought about the night he had with Disncy and wondered if there was a future with her. He looked out the window and saw Murder standing outside of McDonald's.

Murder saw a taxi pull up and the back door open. He saw Scar emerge from the backseat and threw his hands in the air.

"WHAT'S UP! MY NIGGA." Scar shouted, as he walked over and hugged Murder. They walked down the street and stood outside of Walgreens. "I was up at the skating rink last night and I ran into my cousin's brother Blammer from the Point."

"Yeah! What was that nigga talking about?" Murder asked.
"You. He was asking questions about you. He acted like he was trying to get with you but I dead that and told him if he gets with you then he will have to get with me because I had your back."
"That's real nigga shit." Murder said.
"You looked out for me and it's only right that I look out for you by any means." Scar said as he saw a light blue 3 Series BMW ride past.

* * * * * *

"Blammer, what this Nigga Murder look like?" Venom asked.

105

3 Pounds of Pressure 2: When Pressure is Applied

That is the nigga right there, Blammer pointed, as he saw Murder talking to someone, "bust a U-turn. I am about to pop this Nigga," Blammer said as he pulled out his gun.

Venom made a U-turn and drove toward Walgreens. He drove slowly toward them. Venom drove up on Murder and Scar. Blammer pointed the gun out of the window and shouted, "THE POINT BITCH!" and started shooting.
"BOC, BOC, BOC."
Oh shit, Scar said, as he ducked and pulled out his gun. He popped up and pulled the trigger.
"BOOM. BOOM. BOOM. BOOM."

Venom sped forward and turned out of a side street.

"LET ME OUT," Blammer shouted.

Venom pulled over and let Blammer out. Blammer ran up the street and turned the corner and saw Scar and Murder running up the street. He chased them shooting his gun. As they reached the corner Scar turned to shoot back and him and Blammer made eye contact.

"Damn it," Blammer said as he looked at Scar and started backing away.
"I told him to leave it alone, fuck it, now it's on." Scar said as he ran.

Blammer backed up and ran down the side street and hopped in the

BMW, *"I see this bitch ass nigga Scar really got that nigga Murder's back. Damn, now I'm going to have to bring it to him now."*

* * * * * *

Baby Fe sat in her living room talking to Scar's caseworker. She was pissed that her son had not been attending his anger management programs.

"He hasn't made it to the program in the last two months. We are now in the month of July and he hasn't returned any of my calls since May."

"Well. Miss Acres, I will have him call you as soon as I can reach him. I need you to let him know that if he doesn't return my calls that we will not actively pursue him, but the next time he gets arrested for trespassing, disorderly or even jaywalking he wouldn't see the streets until he is twenty-one." Ms. Acres threatened.

"I will let him know that." Baby Fe said, "I *don't trust this bitch,* "Baby Fe thought, as she looked at Miss Acres, "I have to get to work. Ms. Acres." Baby Fe lied, *"Damn, I'm going to have to call my sister and see if my son could stay with her for a while.*

Chapter 16

The evening before Academy's Day Venom and Blammer decided to cruise through the areas controlled by the Academy Homes gang. Blammer sat in the passenger seat while Venom drove down Columbus Avenue heading in the direction of the Academy Homes. Blammer spotted a tall, lanky nigga wearing an Atlanta Braves cap at the bus stop on the corner of Ritchie Street and Columbus Avenue.

"Yo! That's the nigga Scar right there, "Blammer pointed, mistaken the guy at the bus stop as Scar. "Pull over." He ordered.

As Venom stopped. Blammer leaned out the window and yelled. "TWENTY-ONE GUN SALUTE."

The innocent guy at the bus stop saw Blammer leaning out the window with a gun in his hand and tried to run. He didn't get far as the bullets from Blammer's gun hit his neck, shoulder and upper back. Blammer laughed as he thought about the Black Rhinos that filled the clip. What Blammer didn't know was that the person he had killed wasn't Scar and was an honor student named Aaron and the A on his baseball cap stood for his name and not Academy Homes.

Pitt and Scar heard the gunshots from inside the project and thought it was Heath Street. They came running out of the tunnel and saw a car screeching away toward Centre Street. They both looked and saw someone stretched out on the sidewalk and pulled out their guns, ran toward Centre Street and shot at the car. Venom drove the BMW up Centre Street and heard a few gunshots and looked through his rear-view mirror. He saw two niggas shooting their guns.

"Pull over and let me get out," Blammer demanded.
"Nah! Let's get the fuck outta here and come back another time," Venom said, as he drove toward Dudley Street.
"You right, at least I got that nigga Scar. Let's go to the Point and celebrate." Blammer said, "but what he didn't know was if he would have had pulled up a few minutes earlier he would have bumped into Scar.

Pitt and Scar turned around and ran over to where the body was stretched out.
"Who's that?" Pitt asked.

"I don't know, but let's get the fuck outta here dawg," Scar said.

After the shooting Scar and Pitt went to Kia's apartment and laid low. Pitt decided to tell Scar what happened at Academy Day a few years back when Juicy from Heath Street was murdered.

"HEATH STREET IS COMING! HEATH STREET IS COMING!"
A female from the Dark Side shouted.

The activities in the park froze as Pitt and his crew reached for their waist and pulled out their guns. Juicy made it to the park and was met with rapid fire. He backed up and pulled the trigger of the Tec-9. A few shots sputtered out the barrel and the gun jammed. He squeezed the trigger a few more times, turned around and tried to run. His two hundred and eighty-five-pound frame ran in slow motion as he attempted to get away. As he made it a few feet from the car Pitt stepped out of an alley raised a .44 Revolver and pulled the trigger.

"BOOM! BOOM!"

The two shots hit juicy in his back. Juicy's accomplice "Speedy" heard the loud gunshots and saw Juicy crash to the ground. He put the car in drive and sped off leaving Juicy to fend for himself. Juicy cried for help as Pitt walked up on him and placed the .44 to his face. Pitt thought about all the children who were at the park and all the past events that happened by the hands of the Heath Street gang and pulled the trigger.

"BOOM!"

The residents of Academy Homes stood at the top of the hill watching Pitt lay down his murder game. Pitt caught up to his crew looked at them and said.

"That's how you put in work."

"Since that day we been going back and forth with them niggas and we lost some and so did they, but always keep your eyes open because they can attack anytime dawg.

They spoke for hours about possible retaliation from members of the Bromley-Heath Street gang, ways to make Academy one of the most feared gangs in the city and how to stay under the radar of the police.

Chapter 17

The residence of Academy Homes held the annual Academy Day at Marcella Park on the Saturday before Independence Day.

Free watched Scar, Pitt, and a few others walk inside the park and sit on the bleachers. He tapped bully and nodded and pointed to Scar.

"That's the little Nigga who's going to bring his father out of hiding."

Bully stared at Scar and laughed. He knew that the return of Uncle Stretch meant the return of Broad Day Jay. He remembers the day that Broad Day Jay pulled out a machine gun on him and made him piss on himself. That was a day that he would never forget.

"Yo! Tomb, that is our next murder victim," Bully says seriously.

Bully and Tomb were two gangsters who repped the Light Side of the Academy Homes. They looked up to Free and did anything he asked especially Bully. Bully was overweight for his height. At 5 ft 9 and 270 pounds he was considered obese. His stomach protrudes outward which made him look like he was 6 months pregnant. His uneven cornrows stop at the bottom of his ears.

Scar saw Bully staring at him and turned to Pitt and asked, "who's that over there with Free?"

"That's them older niggas from the Light Side. The fat one is Bully and the tall one is Tomb. Those two niggas are Free's puppets."

"What's that on their shirts?" Scar asked. "Every Academy day they each wear 'Free Sincere' t-shirts."

"Who is Sincere?" Scar asked.

"He's Free's younger brother. He's the money maker out of their crew. Sincere been getting big paper in the project since your father left."

"Where is he at? In the Feds?" Scar asked.

"No! He's upstate. He been bagged for a little over three years."

"Oh okay. It's always nice to put faces with names," Scar said, as he stared at Free and his crew. "What do you think about starting our own faction?" Scar asked, changing the subject.

"There is really no need. We are pretty much organized." Pitt answered.

"I see different. For what I had been seeing is that there is no unity in the project. The Light Side niggas rock with Light Side and Dark Side niggas rock with Dark Side niggas. I see loyalty, honor, and dedication, but no unity. We need to bring both sides together as one."

Pitt thought about what scar asked and realized that there wasn't any unity amongst those his age. "What's on your mind?" Pitt inquired.

"I need to know who the top shooters from both sides of the project are, who displays the most loyalty and who is capable of holding a project on its back if need be. I think we should create our own faction of wolves to watch one another's backs and show other gangs in the city how we roll. In other words we need all the dogs under one banner."

Pitt pointed out 12 of the worst in the project. He called Gangster, Hood, Red, Riot, Curly, Slizz, Paul, Allen, Little Barry, Rabbit, Homicide, and Sad over. He looked at Scar and nodded.

Scar cleared his throat and told everyone his reasons on why they should come together as one and call themselves The Wolf Pack. He let each and every one talk, ask questions, and gave them an option to join or not. They all agreed and that's how the Wolfpack was formed.

Free saw Scar and the newly-formed Wolfpack huddled on the bleachers and wondered what was going on.

"Let's see what these little niggas are up to?" Free said, as he led the way towards the bleachers.

"What's up Free?" Pitt said standing up.

"Just enjoying this game, eating some of these hot dogs and

hamburgers. What y'all little niggas up to?" Free asked.

"Just getting things in order. It's up to us to represent the project like y'all did back in the days?" Pitt said.

"I hear that. I thought y'all was plotting and planning over here," Free said, as he stared at scar, "I'm going to let y'all get your little pow wow on," Free laughed, as he walked away. He looked at Bully and said, "keep tabs on that little nigga Scar we going to get at him tonight, when his pops come to his aid he too will be murdered."

Bully nodded his head, but he knew with the return of Uncle Stretch and Broad Day Jay would be a situation that he wasn't ready for.

The rest of Academy day went smooth. After the event Scar went to Kia's apartment with Pitt. They spoke about the rash of shootings that had been happening around the project.

"We have to keep a low profile for a while because with what had just happened with that honor roll kid them D-boys are going to be around here asking questions and searching for clues." Pitt said.

"I'm going to lay low at my mother's house for a few days and let the heat in the project die down. That shit that happened last year with that Heat kid, do think everyone is going to keep their mouth shut? " Scar asked.

"I think so. I would hate to put a few niggas or their family members in the dirt you must look at how everything transpired. I was like a hero out there that day. I basically prevented an innocent bystander from getting shot. Imagine if one of those little kids would have got hit or killed. In the projects we have strict codes of silence."

"That's good to know. I was just asking because I would hate for you to go down for that shit."

"That's the least of my worries right now. I'm focused on getting money and taking care of the family."

"I hear that," Scar said, as he yawned. "I'm about to head home and get some rest," Scar said, as he gave Pitt dap and walked toward the front door.

"You still got the heat?" Pitt asked.

"Yeah!" Scar answered.

"Just checking because those Heath Street niggas might be around here lurking, so be on point. Which way are you going?"

"To the bus stop on Columbus Ave."

"Nah! Those Heath Street niggas might spot you. If I were you, I would catch the bus on Washington Street. That way you will be close to the Light Side."

"Alright," Scar said, as he opened the door and walked out.

Scar walked out of Kia's apartment and saw that the courtyard was empty. He walked to Dimock Street and turned into the Four Squares and disappeared.

He saw Free's Range Rover parked on Washington Street.

"Where's this fuck boy at?" Scar asked himself, as he walked toward Washington Street.

Free and Bully was standing near a dumpster when they spotted Scar turn the corner. Free smiled, pulled out his gun and told Bully to start the Range. Scar looked to his left and saw Bully walking toward the Range Rover. Scar heard a loud gun shot and ducked.

"Oh Shit!" Scar said, as he saw Free running his way with a shiny gun in his hand. Scar reached for his waist and pulled out his gun. "BOOM! BOOM! BOOM!" Three more shots flew out of Free's gun, as he ran toward Scar. Scar got low and ran behind a parked car. He pointed his gun at Free and pulled the trigger. "BOOM! BOOM!"

Free ducked and returned a few more shots in Scar's direction. As he turned around and ran toward the passenger side of his Range Rover a bullet hit his arm. He opened the door and hopped in. "PULL OFF. THIS NIGGA SHOT ME," Free shouted, as he held his arm.

Scar watched the Range Rover speed off and ran to Kia's apartment. *"Damn, shit is getting real out here. It seems like everywhere I go there's drama."* Scar said to himself, as he thought about the shoot-out, he had with Blammer, *"I have to get my shit straight, because next time I see Free I'm going to kill him."* Scar thought, as he knocked on Kia's door. She opened the door and Scar walked into the apartment and told Pitt what had just happened and how he had to lay low until the morning. Scar stayed up the rest of the night talking to Pitt until Curly came in the morning. Scar explained to Curly what had happened with Free.

"You good dawg?" Curly asked.

"Yeah! I'm good. I need to clear my head," Scar said, as him, Pitt and Curly walked outside. "I'm about to bounce. I'll see y'all later." Scar said, as he gave them dap.

"Be safe and keep your eyes open." Pitt said.

"No doubt." Scar said, as he walked out of the project and toward the taxi stand.

Chapter 18

A black Cadillac Escalade pulled up and the door popped open. Nastee stepped out and saw all the people he grew up with and smiled.

"Home Sweet Home," he said, as he scanned the faces in the crowd looking for his son.

It's been a little over ten years and while Nastee was in state prison he heard that his younger son Byron was attempting to follow in his footsteps, and this angered Nastee because he was already hurting about the loss of his son and he wanted better for the last son he had left. He knew that there were only a few exits from the streets, and he had to get to him before the streets fully swallowed him up and spit him out, but what Nastee didn't know was that his son was already fully engulfed into the streets and he also had attempted murders and murders under his belt.

Byron "Nastee" Collins was born and raised in Dorchester's Columbia Point Housing Project. At a young age, his mother abandoned him and left him in the care of his grandmother. It was his grandmother who had raised him, but by the time Nastee turned fourteen, he started to venture out in the streets. He found the love he was searching for through two brothers from Detroit, Michigan.

Mud and his little brother Dirt left Detroit in search for a new city to move their heroin. They found it in Boston's burgeoning heroin trade through a female from Columbia Point and through her they were introduced to the gangsters who ran the project. Their first week in the project they were approached by a sixteen-year-old kid named Byron wanting to get down. They listened to his pleas as he expressed how he wanted to instill fear and have people across the city respect him and his crew opposed to getting money. The two brothers took up the kid's offer and decided to bring him back to Detroit and show him how the Murder City got down. Therein Detroit young Byron learned how to enhance his murder game by watching gruesome acts of violence. It was there where young Byron earned the name Nastee because of the way he murdered victims in the behest of mud and dirt.

When he came back, he was too much for the streets of Boston to handle. His uncontrollable ways, ill temper, and violent mentality were the main traits that had propelled him to great success. His success stemmed from the moves he had made in the streets. His kill at will attitude and the fear he instilled in others allowed him to extort several hustlers for thousands of dollars every week. The money he made from hustling and extortion was used to buy several houses in Dorchester and a barbershop in South Boston. He was also an obsessive taskmaster who worked people as if they were his slaves. He wanted and needed results and nothing else.

In Boston's underworld, there were no other living beings who had more murders than him. His ability to orchestrate death had taken a legendary aura in the streets. His enemies feared him, his crew loved him, and his allies respected him. He wore the reputation like a lapel on a coat with honor. His ways were always on the offense and he never let up.

Throughout his years of causing mayhem in the city of Boston, Nastee kept in contact with his mentors from Detroit. Mud returned to Boston and tried to open a heroin operation in the Academy Homes. The gangsters in Academy Homes made it hard for Mud; they shot at him every time he tried to sell heroin in the project. The last time he stepped foot in Academy Homes he was shot in the leg and was left with a limp. Nastee took up Mud's beef with the Academy Homes as his own and exacted revenge. On one occasion he went through Academy Homes shooting and was chased by the police, arrested and charged with attempted murder.

Since Nastee's arrest Mud sporadically came back to Boston and tutored those who were from Nastee's crew and supplied guns and drugs to them. After nine months of waiting trial Nastee was convicted and sentenced to serve a 10 to 12-year sentence in state prison.

Venom drove up Mt. Vernon and parked in the church parking lot. Him and Blammer got out and walked across the street into the Columbia Point Projects.

Blammer spoke to his father and learned that the residents in the projects were throwing a cook-out for his homecoming. He couldn't wait, he had a lot to tell his father about all that he had been through in the past decade. He knew his father had a notorious reputation, but he didn't know to what magnitude his father would go to exact revenge or about the strong ties he had to killers in Detroit. Blammer saw his father walking toward and emerged from the crowd and gave him a hug.

"What's up dad?" Blammer greeted, as he hugged his father, "welcome home. I have so much to tell you. I don't know where to begin."

"We'll talk in private later. There's a few things I want to talk to you about also," Nastee said, as he looked at his son in the eyes.

"Okay." Blammer said.

Nastee walked over to the crowd and shook hands, gave hugs to all the young members and those he grew up with. After he finished talking with Terrible Trav and a few others he grew up with he pulled his son to the side and they walked down to the Gazebo.

"Over the years your mother been telling me about some of the things you haven't been telling me. I know how it is growing up out here and the things you must do to survive, but creating a name is more than just busting a gun. You got to make the right choices at the wrong times and you can't be a follower. There are better ways to do things and going in and out of jail is not the way. I wish I knew the things I know now because I would have not had done half of the things I've done. I fucked up back in the days. I was so feared that I thought no-one would ever have the balls to snitch on me, but they did and got me out of the way for ten years. I want you to learn from those mistakes I made. Those ten years was hard for me. I lost your mother, older brother and missed out on most of your childhood. See, son in prison your at your lowest point. I wasn't even able to go pay my last respect to your brother Faury. How you think that made me feel? I felt like shit, but a good thing happened to me when the state transferred me out of state because I was beginning to self-destruct in Shirley Max. When I went to New Mexico I met a few good people who gave me the links that I need. What I need you to do is fall under the radar, focus on making money and don't make the same mistakes that I made. You are still young and have a future ahead of you. What are your plans? Do you have any?"

"Yeah! I mess with this music thing. This is my ticket out of the hood."

"I heard that you were making music. How long you been into that?" Nastee asked.

"I been making music since I was thirteen. Me, my man Cool and his

126

brother Flip formed a group that we call Eight-Bus huh!"

"Yeah! We decided to pay homage to the bus route that ends in the point. We made a few mix C.D.'s and did a few shows around the town, but outside of New England we are unknown. We make good music, but we need a push."

"What kind of push are you talking about?"

"Coast to coast that international action."

"Well, one of my friends owns a Hip Hop magazine and I can see if I can get you an interview and some advertising."

"Word dad, that's what's up. I appreciate that. We need that push. I want to make this money out here and put the P on the map. I'm a Point nigga to the death of me." Blammer said.

"Byron, the game is bigger than what you think. I'm not going to try to stop you from doing what you want to do in these streets, but I don't want you to look back and wish you would've used the talents you have. I want you to think about every move you decide to make because the moves you make today will decide your future. If you decide to rep the Point then rep it right, make music and put the Point on the map in the Hip Hop world and leave all the bullshit alone."

"That's what I wanted to talk to you about." Blammer said.

"Okay. About what?" Nastee asked.

"The bullshit. We are beefing with damn near every hood in the city and holding it down. We have a strong unity and bond in the project that's unbreakable."

"I hear you son. But if you want to get money be the sole controller and not the one being controlled. You have a good thing going for you with the music. Capitalize from it and get money. I have no problem with showing you how to be the sole controller of those around you, keep me posted with what's going on."

"Since you been down niggas from the Point branched out and started hustling in Maine, Connecticut, Vermont, New Hampshire, Taunton, and Rhode Island."

"I heard that and that is a good thing to spread your wings. Those niggas who hustle elsewhere can be avenues for you to promote your music. I will show you how to organize your crew and use everyone to your advantage. It's like playing chess, you must have all the pawns protect you. I must make a few moves out of the state and when I get back, we will make moves together. Until then just stay under the radar."

Blammer listened to his father and decided to keep the problem he had with Scar between him and his crew. He walked over to his crew and rounded them up and explained to them his reasons for going to war with Scar and those who had Scar's back.

Chapter 19

Scar sat on a stoop outside a building on Regent Street and called Mia. Scar finished the call and he knew if anyone knew what happened it was Pitt. He dialed Pitt's number and learned about the death of the honor student and how the shooter fled in a light blue three series BMW. Scar knew that the shooter was Blammer and his crew. Scar knew next time he saw Blammer it was kill or be killed. He finished the call with Pitt and walked down the street and spotted a taxi and flagged it down. He got in the taxi and directed the driver to Mia's house.

"Damn, this nigga Blammer and Free tried to get at me. I gotta keep my eyes open," Scar thought, as the taxi pulled up outside of Mia's

condominium. He paid the fare, stepped out and walked to her front door. He knocked three times and placed his hand in his pocket and gripped the Ruger P89.

Mia heard the knocks, looked through the peep-hole, and saw Scar. She opened the door and saw the grim look on his face. *"Damn, I swear this nigga look familiar. Where the hell I know this nigga from?"* Mia asked herself.

"What's up beautiful," Scar said, as he gave Mia a hug.

"I'm glad that you made it," Mia said, as she stepped out of the way and allowed him into her house.
Scar looked in every room before joining Mia in the living room.

"Nobody's here. I'm not one of those bitches who have all types of niggas in my house."
"How I know that?" Scar asked.
"Trust and believe me if you stick around, you'll see. I'm a rare breed. I made something to eat are you hungry?"
"I'm good thanks. I ate a little earlier." Scar said, as he sat down on the couch and looked Mia in her eyes. "I'm real secretive. A lot of shit happened in my past that left me paranoid and not trusting too many people. I want to ask you a question. How many people know you live here?"
"Just my family and a few of my friends. I don't let too many people know where I rest my head."

"That's good to know." Scar said, as he managed to crack a smile, "So I'm safe here?"

"Yeah!" Mia answered, "You look familiar. I saw you somewhere before?"

"You probably know my mother." Scar said.

"Who's your mother?" Mia asked.

"Baby Fe." Scar answered.

"Fesal, from Castlegate?" Mia asked.

"Yeah! You know her?"

"Do I know her! Boy, I remember the day you were born. So, Uncle Stretch is your father?"

"Yeah! That's my old man."

"I knew you looked familiar. I remember your spoiled ass," Mia said, as she thought about all the media coverage Scar garnered in the past, "How is your mother doing?"

"Good. She is working as a nurse."

"I heard she was a nurse. That's good, tell her that Mia said what's up."

"Alright. How long you been living here?"

"A few months. This development is new."

"Where's your boyfriend?"

"I don't have one, because a lot of these niggas be fake as hell. They tell you one thing and do the other.

Scar grabbed Mia's hand and kissed it. She slid over and cuddled with him. "Come on. I know you didn't come here to cuddle there's no reason to be shy" she said, as she unbuttoned her pants and pulled them down.

Scar saw that Mia had on no panties. His dick got hard as he watched her step out of her pants one leg at a time. She sat back on the couch, spread her legs, grabbed his hand and placed it on her pussy. He rubbed his index and middle finger over her outer lips and then started rubbing the clit. He felt her clit swell up and pulled back and took off his shirt and placed it on the edge of the couch.

Mia saw the gun in his waist and shook her head. He grabbed the gun, placed it on the dining table and kicked off his sneakers. He grabbed a condom out of his pocket, unbuttoned his jeans, and pulled them down to his ankles. Mia stepped up, turned around and placed her hands on the arm rest. He put on the condom, stepped closer and placed his dick inside of her and started pumping hard. Mia moaned as he stroked hard and fast. After about five minutes he flipped her over and started banging her out missionary style. It took about seven minutes for Scar to cum. After they finished sexing, he got up, pulled up his pants and grabbed his gun. He walked to the bathroom and cleaned himself. He liked everything about Mia's place and wanted to spend more time with her. He decided to make it his getaway spot. He stepped back in the living room and sat next to her.

"So, what's on the agenda?" Mia asked.

"Just time. I want to spend these next few days getting to know more about you."

"I'm down with that," Mia said, as she placed her head on his chest, "so tell me more about your past?"

"Be easy. In time you will learn all you want to know about me." Scar said.

Chapter 20

While Scar was spending time at Mia's he told her everything from the case that had sent him to the Department of Youth Services, his heroin use, and his reasons for trusting no-one. Mia assured him that he could trust her and if he wanted, he could move in. Scar decided that he would use her house to fall back and gather his thoughts. He hugged and kissed her and left. He took a taxi to the Dark Side and saw Pitt and Riot standing outside of Kia's apartment. As he approached his crew, he saw an older head walking toward them with a bag in his hand.

Scar studied the older head and asked. "Who's that?"
Pitt hunched his shoulders. Scar pulled up his T-shirt and revealed the butt of a .9mm Ruger and shouted, "YO! MY MAN, WHO YOU

KNOW IN HERE?"

The older head stopped and looked at all the Braves' hats. *"Damn, I hope these little niggas remember my family,"* the older head thought.

"COME HERE." Pitt shouted. The older head hesitated and then stepped toward them.

"You heard my man. Who you came to see?" Riot said, stepping forward.

"My family." The older head answered.

"Who's your family?" Pitt asked.

"I'm Murphy. Where's Uncle Stretch, Broad Day Jay, and the twins Trauma and Drama at?"

The older said nervously.

"Why?" Scar asked. "Who are you?"

"I'm Fresh Eddie. I'm from around here. I had just been living out of town for some years."

"Where at?" Pitt asked.

"Damn, these little niggas asking questions like they are the feds," Fresh Eddie thought, "I live in Maine."

Pitt instantly thought about the pipeline of guns that funnel through the states of Maine and New Hampshire.

"Let's take a walk, Fresh Eddie," Scar said.

Fresh Eddie walked with Scar to Ritchie Street and stopped. "Stretch is my father and he's been gone for a decade. So, what's your real business here?" Scar asked, as he pulled the Ruger from his waist and placed it to Fresh Eddie's neck. "Matter of fact, I'm going to call him and if he says anything negative it's off with ya' head."

"Hold on youngblood. Your Baby Fe's son?"

"Yeah!" Scar answered.

"Well call her." Fresh Eddie said

"Nah! I'm calling my dad." Scar said.

"Listen. I'm here just trying to sell some of these guns and go on my way." Fresh Eddie said.

"What kind of guns?" Scar asked as he let go of Fresh Eddie's collar and stepped back.

"I have Taurus's, Berettas, and Colts." Fresh Eddie answered.

"In that bag?" Scar pointed.

"Yeah!"

"Drop that bag," Scar demanded.

Fresh Eddie did as he was told. He looked at Scar and saw the same uni-brow that Uncle Stretch had. *"Damn, this nigga looks just like his pops."*

Scar pulled out his phone and dialed his father number. He asked his father about Fresh Eddie and once it was confirmed that he was official, and a solid gun connect he hung up and looked at Fresh Eddie in the eyes and said. "My dad said that you are one of us. How many guns you have in that bag?"

"Six. Four nine millimeters, and two four-fives." Fresh Eddie answered.

"How much you want for them guns?"

"With the project discount, two hundred apiece for the nine millimeters and three hundred for the four-fives."

Scar reached in his pocket and pulled out some money and passed it to him. Fresh Eddie counted the money and nodded his head.

"My bad for pointing a gun at you. I hope that you understand my reasons on how I roll in these streets, no one is to be trusted."

"I understand young blood."

"What else can you get besides handguns?"

"Anything. Matter of the facet, at my niece's apartment I have a bullet-proof vest and a couple of Mac-tens."

"Who's your niece?" Scar asked.

"Strawberry." Fresh Eddie.

"Good shit," Scar said, as he thought about the day Strawberry broke his virginity. "Whatever you have there I want."

Fresh Eddie looked at Scar and wanted to ask him who he was at war with. "Alright. Let's take a walk to my niece's apartment."

They walked to Strawberry's apartment. Scar followed him into the building and walked up the stairs. Fresh Eddie knocked on the door three times. The door flung open and Strawberry stepped aside and allowed them in. Scar greeted her and walked in the living room. Fresh Eddie grabbed a bag from beside the couch and zipped it open. Scar watched as he pulled out a bullet-proof vest, two Mac-10's, two shoulder holsters, a box of bullets and two extra clips. Scar looked at the vest and smiled.

"That's a level two Kevlar vest," Fresh Eddie informed.

Scar took off his shirt and strapped on the vest. He reached in the bag and grabbed a .45 Colt, a .9mm Beretta and a .9mm Taurus. He placed the Taurus on his waist and the Colt and Beretta in shoulder holsters. "I need a sweater or something to conceal this shit." Scar said, as he stared at Fresh Eddie.

"Hold up, the last time I came here I left a couple hooded sweatshirts." Fresh Eddie said, as he walked inside of a bedroom. He came back out a minute later holding a navy-blue Champion hooded sweatshirt. "Here you go." He said, as he handed it to Scar.

"What I owe you for these guns?"
"The submachine guns go for five hundred apiece and the vest is two hundred. Since you are Uncle Stretch's son give me a stack and you can have it all the holsters, bullets, and the extra clips as well."

"Good looking out." Scar said, as he pulled out some money and counted a thousand dollars. He handed the money to Fresh Eddie and exchanged information with him. He placed the Mac-tens and boxes of bullets in the bag and looked at Fresh Eddie. "Let me ask you a question dawg, where did you get all these guns from?"

"I own an armory in Maine." Fresh Eddie answered.

"What's an armory?"

"It's a gun store."

"Word." Scar said with excitement in his voice.

"Yeah! Every now and then I order a few extra guns and show love to the hood."

"Damn, you are a good nigga." Scar said, as he walked out of the apartment. He walked out of the building and into the courtyard toward where Riot and Pitt stood. "I just came up with some nice joints. Take this bag to Kia's," Scar said to Pitt and he handed Pitt the bag.

Pitt grabbed the bag, opened it and saw the two Mac-tens and gave Scar and Riot dap and walked toward Kia's apartment. Scar finally had a solid gun connect and now all he had to do was take a trip to Maine and order some assault-rifles. He knew he had to show one person love. "Riot, can you take me to Codman Square to see my man Murder."

Chapter 21

Riot drove to Codman Square and Scar saw Murder and a few members of his crew standing outside of an apartment building.

"Right here," Scar said.

Murder saw the Mercedes-Benz pull to a stop and stepped beside a car, reached under it and pulled out a .45 Ruger.

"Who's that?" One of Murder's boys asked.

"I don't know, but they are about to get aired out." Murder said, as he saw Scar step out of the passenger door. "That's my dawg Scar from Academy," Murder said with a smile on his face.

Scar stepped toward them with his hands in his pocket. "Murder 187 what's good?" Scar asked, as he approached Murder and gave him dap. "I have a gift for you, come on let's take a walk."

Murder and Scar walked halfway down the street and stopped near a house.

"What's good?" Murder asked. "This," Scar said, as he pulled a Beretta from his pocket.
"That's what I'm talking about nigga. I love guns." Murder said with a smile.

Scar passed Murder the Beretta. Murder took out the clip and inspected it and inserted it back in.

"What I owe you?" Murder asked.
"Nothing. You my nigga and I always look out for my niggas. You did me a favor when I was in need so when I came up, I thought about you first."
"Good looking out dawg."

Scar gave Murder the three-finger handshake and walked up the street and slid in the Mercedes-Benz. Riot pulled off and drove down Talbot Avenue and took a left on Blue Hill Avenue.

* * * * * *

Disney had her hair flat past her shoulders, on her bubble butt was some ashy, black jeans. She crossed the intersection of Blue Hill Avenue and Morton Street. The sounds of a honking horn and screeching tires made her jump. She looked around her shoulders and saw a blue Honda Accord.

"GET THE FUCK OUTTA THE STREET BITCH," yelled the disrespectful driver of the Honda.

The driver wore a New York Giants jersey. It didn't take a rocket scientist to know that he was from Franklin Hill Project. The gangsters in that project wore both the New York and San Francisco Giants.

Disney stood in the middle of the street and gave him the middle finger salute.

"YOU STINK BITCH," he shouted.

Disney ignored him and walked across the street and stepped onto the crowded sidewalk. Two cars behind the Honda sat Riot's Mercedes.

"Yo! Scar isn't that the little bitch you bagged at the Vous?"

Scar leaned up on his elbows and lifted his Atlanta Braves cap to get a better look. They watched as Disney crossed Blue Hill Ave and stepped on the sidewalk. They watched her turn around, spot the Mercedes and spin on her heels. Disney was afraid to associate with

Scar after the ass kicking that she had received from her man. She hoped that Clapper still wasn't at the corner of Leston Street. Her Stuart Weitzman heels click, clacked, on the hot pavement as she walked down Morton Street.

"YO! DISNEY! YO! DISNEY!" Riot yelled.

Disney kept her head straight and walked down the street. Her heart raced as she made it to the corner of Leston Street. She looked down Lucerne and sighed relief that Clapper and his boys were gone.

"YO! DISNEY," Riot yelled. "You sure that's the bitch?" he asked Scar.
"Yeah! That's her."

Disney looked at the Mercedes and pointed to a parking lot. Riot sped forward and parked in the lot. Scar jumped out, walked across the lot and leaned on a wrought-iron fence. He watched Disney cross the street and grabbed her hand. She looked around and gave him a nervous hug. He wondered why she was acting so jittery. They walked to the Mercedes and Disney climbed into the back seat and sunk low. Scar looked through the mirror and asked her was she alright. She shook her head and stared out the window.

"I see you never called me," Scar said.
"You got my number," Disney replied.

Disney sat in the back and remained quiet for the rest of the ride. Riot pulled into the parking lot of Eblens and parked. Scar opened the door and waited for Disney. They walked a few feet from the car then she leaned in for a hug. He grabbed her ass cheeks and kissed her on the forehead. Riot joined them and they walked into the store. Riot stopped at the Timberland section while Scar and Disney walked to the Adidas section. Scar picked up a pair of black on black Top Ten Adidas and showed it to the store manager. When she walked in the back, Scar turned to Disney and looked at her light freckles and ran the back of his hand over her face. The store manager came out with a blue Adidas box and walked toward the cash register. Riot was already at the cash register with a pair of construction Timberlands. Disney leaned on her toes and stuck her tongue into Scar's ear and swirled it around. While she was giving his ear fellatio, three girls stepped in the store. All three of the girls had on Washington Nationals' Baseball caps. The W on the caps stood for Wildwood Street. The darkest one out of the three pointed.

"DISNEY," Lisha shouted.

Disney heard her girls Lisha squeaky voice, turned around and almost had a heart attack as she spotted her crew. She gave them a double take and turned back to Scar.

Scar stared at the three girls who had betrayal written all over their faces.

147

"Those niggas must be from Academy," Clapper's sister Mary said, as she saw that Scar and Riot had on Atlanta Braves caps.

"That A better stand for Almont Park," Disney hissed.

The three girls stormed over toward Disney and stopped. Mary looked Scar up and down and curled her lip at him.

"Where are you from?" Mary asked.

"Academy Terror Homes." Scar answered.

"This bitch done lost her mind. You fucking with a Roxbury nigga, you better not let your man catch you," Lisha blurted out.

"Who these dirty bitches?" Riot asked, as he walked over.

"Dirty. Please nigga no one from Wildwood is dirty." Mary said.

Disney stood there frozen. She couldn't believe her luck when it came to Scar. The thought of Clapper finding out was enough to turn her stomach.

"YO! DISNEY YOU KNOW THAT'S CONSIDERED TREASON. BITCH, YOU BETTER NOT LET CLAPPER CATCH YOU." Daisy shouted.

"Bitch don't let this get back to the hood, you know Clapper's her man!" Mary warned.

Riot had enough, "look you dirty bitches need to get somewhere before I get mad. Fuck you, your hood and fuck Clapper, you dirty hood rat bitches."

"Fuck you sucker ass niggas," Mary said, and then turned to Disney, "I'm telling my brother about this."

Disney lowered her head and walked out of the store. Scar followed her and asked. "Are you rolling with us or going with them?"

"I have no choice but to roll with y'all," Disney said with sadness in her voice.

"What was all that about?" Scar asked.

"Nothing," Disney said with her head down.

"You good?" Riot asked, as he came out of the store. "I'm sorry for disrespecting your friends, but they were trying to diss my hood.

"Yeah! I'm good. I have to keep it real, the reason why I didn't call was because after we hooked up, I went home, and my man found out that we hooked up and he beat the shit out of me. He fucked me up. I was scared. My man is crazy. His name is Clapper."

Scar raised his left eyebrow because he knew who she was talking about. They were in juvenile detention together and even back then Clapper was jealous of Scar for all the flavored Adidas that Scar had. *"Damn, she fuck with that lunatic,"* Scar thought.

"You will be good. Don't sweat it," Riot said, as he unlocked the doors to the Mercedes.

Disney wiped away the tears with the back of her hand and slid in the back seat. She squirmed showing discomfort. Riot put the car in drive and pulled off. He saw the trio walking toward the bus stop. He drove toward them, rolled down the window and stuck up his middle finger.

Disney closed her eyes because she knew that he had just added more fuel to the fire. She stared out the window and thought about her next move. She was scared shitless of her man and what he was going to do to her when he caught her. Riot drove to Shandon Road and Disney saw the bricks that made up Franklin Hill Project. He parked near a set of benches, reached in the arm rest and grabbed a glass jar of weed. Disney and Scar stepped out and walked toward the group sitting on the benches. The next half hour they smoked blunt after blunt. Disney's eyes were on chink status from the amount of weed she had just inhaled. They stepped back in the car and Disney was starting to feel horny. Her phone vibrated, she looked at the text.

"Disney, Clapper got bagged with a tone," the text read.

Disney felt relieved that her ass kicking was now on hold for a few months. She looked out the window and nodded to the music. She leaned her body forward and whispered in Scar's ear. "Let's go to Kia's."

Chapter 22

Disney woke Scar up with a kiss. He took his time getting up. He got out of the bed and walked to the window. He looked out the window into the courtyard and watched Disney getting into a taxi. The night before was filled with raw unprotected sex. He washed his face and brushed his teeth. He pulled out a bag of heroin, opened it and snorted a few lines. It was a quarter to eight and he was ready to start his day. He stepped out into the courtyard and headed toward St. Joseph.

* * * * * *

Across the street from the Ritchie Street entrance of Academy Homes two men sat in a blue Toyota Camry with two-ways in their hands. Bully looked out the passenger window while Tomb kept his eyes on

Marcella Street. Bully had in his lap a fully loaded .9mm Ruger. He saw Scar come out of the project, look to his left and then turned down a side street. Bully raised his two-way and alerted Free. Free was wearing a dread wig and sunglasses. He always disguises himself when he put in work because if he's spotted the witness would give a false description to the authorities. He received the chirp from Bully, tapped Wyonna on the thigh and nodded. Wyonna opened the door, stepped out the passenger seat and headed down Thornton Street. Her plan was to distract Scar and shoot him from behind. Free prepped her on the job and knew with her exotic features she could pull it off.

Wyonna was a half Italian/Jamaican female from Randolph. Free met her at a club in Stoughton, Ma called Alex's. He knew with her green eyes, hour-glass shape and long curly hair that she could make lots of money. He told her what she wanted to hear and eventually persuaded her to work as an escort.

Scar walked up the street looking at all the parked cars and spotted an unfamiliar face walking toward him. It was just them two this quiet morning. The female had her arms folded across her chest. Scar noticed how beautiful she was and how he could see all her curves in her stretch pants. Scar knew the street was usually empty in the morning and found the pretty female appearance unusual. "*Who the fuck is this bitch?*" Scar thought, as he walked past her. He looked back to see the shape of her ass and noticed her spinning back. He immediately sensed danger as his survival instincts kicked in. "*I knew something wasn't right,* "Scar said, as he reached his hand in his waist

153

and pulled out his .45 Colt and turned around.

Wyonna spun around to reveal a .380 Bryco. She raised the gun and pulled the trigger.

"BOC! BOC!"
The first two shots whizzed past Scar. He ducked and raised his gun and pulled the trigger.
"BOOM! BOOM! BOOM!"

The first three shots crashed into her chest plate and lifted her off the ground. Tomb heard the exchange of gunshots and sensed something was wrong. He drove to Thornton Street. Bully hopped out of the Camry and turned the corner. He saw Scar backing away and pulled the trigger.

"BOOM! BOOM! BOOM! BOOM!"

Scar took cover behind a parked car, raised his hand and returned fire. He hopped up and ran in the street and fired two shots. Bully ducked and started to run backward as he raised his gun and squeezed off three shots. Scar darted from the street, turned and blew two more shots at Bully and then hopped a small fence. He reached in his back pocket and extracted an extra clip. He discarded the previous clip and placed the new one in the Colt.

Free heard the shoot-out from the street over. "Damn, this silly bitch done fucked up," he said, as he hit the gas pedal. He pushed the pedal to the metal and soon as he turned the corner, he saw Scar hop over a small fence. He rolled down the window, hit the brakes and noticed Scar had his back facing the street behind the fence. Free leaned out the window, raised his gun and let off a volley of shots from his .9mm into Scar's back. He watched Scar fall flat on his face to the ground.

"TIME TO CELEBRATE!" Free shouted.

Chapter 23

Free drove up the street and saw Bully pick up Wynona's gun. Free hit the brakes. The car came to a screeching halt. Bully saw Free, ran over to the car, opened the door and hopped in. Free hit the combination to his secret compartment.

"I just aired that little bitch out," Free said, as he placed the guns in the compartment.

"You think that niggas dead?" Bully asked nervously.

"Yeah!" Free answered.

Bully chirped Tomb and told him to meet them at the stash house on Townsend Street. Free had a stash house on Townsend Street. This was where they discussed business, stashed guns, drugs, and planned their next acts of violence. Free pulled up to the stash house, hopped out and left the keys in the ignition. He dashed into the house. He saw Tomb in the house and gave him the nod. Tomb rushed out of the house past Bully, hopped in the car and sped off.

Tomb's role was to get rid of the dirty gun that was left in the secret compartment and torch the car. He drove to Franklin Park and pulled behind Shattuck hospital. He grabbed the guns, stepped out, walked over to the pond and tossed them in the water. He walked back to the Camry, grabbed a can of gasoline, poured it inside the car, lit a book of matches and tossed it in the backseat of the car.

* * * * * *

A small crowd huddled around the fence where Scar's body laid. His eyes popped open and he started to move his legs; his vision was blurry and couldn't make out the people staring at him. He rolled to his right side where his empty clip laid and sat up. He spotted his gun near the fence and started to panic. He knew the gun was used to shoot the girl. He took ahold of the fence as leverage to stand. He bent down, picked up his clip, wobbled over and grabbed his gun. He placed it in his waist and slowly walked away for the hushed voices. His first instinct was to run but decided to walk to the corner. He hit the corner and jogged down Marcella Park. His body ached from the hits that the vest endured. He reached the bleachers, stashed the gun in the dirt and climbed to the top. He leaned back and closed his eyes thinking if he wasn't high he would've recognized the set up from the start.

"I got to give this dope up before I get killed."

The crowd who stood over Scar's body walked down the street and stared at Wyonna as she laid in a pool of her own blood. Her eyes stared at the sun. The first shot from the gun penetrated her heart killing her instantly. With no fingerprints in the data system they would have to identify her by the dental records.

Scar managed enough strength and walked over to Kia's apartment and knocked on the door.

"What's up Scar?" Kia asked, as she gave him a hug. "Pitt's not here. He went somewhere a little earlier." She said, as she noticed how Scar had grunted when she hugged him. "Are you okay?" She said noticing he walked as if he was in pain.

"Yeah! I'm good. Nah! I'm not! Niggas just tried to kill me on my way to St. Joes and I ended up getting into a crazy shoot-out on Thornton Street." Scar said, as he remembered the crowd that surrounded Wynona's lifeless body. *"Never bring a girl to a gangster party."* Scar thought.

"Who tried to kill you?" Kia asked, as she shut the door and locked it. "Do you know who did it?"

"I don't know. It could have been anybody."

"Damn, you need to lay low."

"I need to get the fuck away from around here," Scar said, as he thought about the girl he shot, "I need a bag to put these guns in."

Kia walked into the kitchen and came back out with a bag. She tossed the bag to Scar. He caught it and asked for the Mac-10, the .9mm Taurus, and two extra clips. She went into the room and Scar reached under the couch and grabbed his .380 and tucked it in his waist. Kia came back out with the guns and the clips.

"Could you call me a taxi?" Scar asked, "thanks for letting me rest here. I found a spot to lay my head."
"You're welcome," Kia said, as she called a taxi.

After Kia called the taxi, she decided to call Pitt to let him know what had happened and that Scar came to grab the guns. A few minutes later a taxi pulled up and Scar stepped out and slid in the backseat. He gave the driver Mia's address and wondered who was behind his assassination attempt. Since it was close to the project, he figured it was Free. *"I'm done with this heroin shit. Fucked around and almost got killed."* Scar thought.

The taxi pulled up to Mia's condominium. Scar paid the fare, opened the door and stepped out. He walked up the stairs and knocked three times. A few minutes later Mia opened the door and the look on Scar's face showed that something had happened.

"What's wrong? I hope you didn't bring no bullshit to the house?" Mia asked, as she wondered why Scar had a hoodie on in the summertime. "I won't ever bring no bullshit to your house, but you are not going to believe what just happened to me," Scar said, as he took off his hoodie and walked inside of her house.

Scar unstrapped his vest and that's when Mia saw all the dents in the vest and knew what happened. She looked at him with a worried look and now knew why he wore the hooded sweatshirt it was to conceal the bullet-proof vest he had on.

"Baby are you alright?"
"Yeah! I'm good. This house is too bright we need to paint it darker. I want black blinds and the walls painted black. Everything must be black," Scar said, as he pulled out a stack of bills and tossed them on the table. "That should take care of everything."

Mia grabbed the bills, her car keys and left to go to Home Depot. He watched from the window as she got in her car and pulled off. When she was gone, he reached in the bag and pulled out the Mac-10, Taurus, the two extra clips and walked into Mia's room. He lifted the mattress and placed the Mac-10 under it. He walked to the bathroom and placed the Taurus and the extra clips in the window seal.

"If this bitch touches these guns; I'm killing everyone she knows." Scar said, as he began to think about all he was going through and how he was going to combat the attacks on his life with violence of his own, *"whoever I got into it with today knew my route and they probably know where I hustle at. Fuck that. My life is worth more than a few thousand dollars."* He thought.
A few hours later Mia came home and saw Scar sitting in the living room with a hood on his head. She saw on the table a .380 handgun.

She placed the bags down on the floor and walked over to the couch and sat next to him. She cozied up with him and laid her head on his chest.

"Hey baby, did you find everything I requested?"

"Yes."

"Good. Because we are going to start painting this living room. I have a few stacks for new furniture. We going to get this shit right. I want to tell you more about me. I don't know your back history or the quality of guys you dealt with in the past, but I just want you to know that I play by a set of different rules. I'm out here trying to get money but keep running into problems. I almost got killed this morning and don't even know who was shooting at me." He said.

"Boy, what you mean you don't know who tried to kill you. You have that many enemies already? You just came out of jail and got beef. You need to slow down and continue getting money. Whatever you do, I'm a ride with you."

"If you ride with me then we are good. If you cross me then you will be slumped. I'm just being honest. There's no cut cards with me." Scar said.

"I told you I'm a rare breed and got your back. Just show me the way," Mia said in return.

"Let me show you what I scattered around the house. But, before any of that I want you out of them clothes. I want you walking around naked when I come here."

Mia smiled, stepped up, and started stripping. Scar watched closely and felt a soft spot for the old head. As she stripped, he got up walked to the window seal and showed her the Taurus and then they walked into the living room and he reached under the mattress and pulled out the Mac-10.

"I'm here for the next few days," Scar said, as he stared at her naked body.

"Good. Come over here and let me give you some of this super head." Mia said.

* * * * * * *

Free watched the news and was pissed that Wyonna was the only one murdered. He listened as one of the witnesses stated that a young man, picked up a gun and walked down the street. He knew somehow Scar had survived the attack on his life.

"I aired the nigga out. How the fuck did he survive that shit." Free said to Bully.

"The bitch nigga had to have a vest on," Free growled, and vowed that next time he bumped heads with Scar, he would make sure, that he would be a dead man. No one survives head shots." Free snarled.

Bully shook his head at how infatuated Free was with killing Scar. "Do you think he knew it was us gunning at him?" Bully asked.

"Doubt it. He might think it was Heath Street or Orchard Park. I have to get him." Free said, as he stood up and looked Bully in his eyes.

163

"That little nigga shot me, killed my bitch Wyonna, and survived both attempts on his life. Three strikes you're out and next time I catch his bitch ass I'm giving him the whole clip to the face."

Chapter 24

The first week Scar spent at Mia's house he used her car to learn how to drive and once he was satisfied with his driving skills, he went to the registry of motor vehicles and took the test to obtain his permit. He passed the test and set up an appointment to take the road test. Two weeks later he took the road test and passed and had his license.

"Now that I have my license, I need to find a new block to hustle and get money on." Scar thought.

Pitt kept Scar up to date with all the happenings in the hood and how the Boston Police "Youth Violence Strike Force" had the project on lock down due to the recent rash of violence. Scar knew he had to keep his distance from his housing project and lay low until he figured things out.

"I'm about to go home and spend some time with my moms," Scar said, as he kissed Mia on the cheek and left. He took the bus to Roxbury Crossing and got on the train and took it to Back Bay Station and connected to the commuter rail. While on the train he decided it was wise to put his hustling in St. Joes on hold. *"It's too risky. My life is worth more than a couple stacks."* He thought.

The train stopped and Scar got off and walked to his house. He pulled out his key, opened the door and walked up the stairs. He opened the door and walked inside. He saw a manila envelope addressed to him. He opened the envelope and saw it was from the Financial Aid office. "Damn, I forgot about this shit." Scar said, as he read the paper and noticed that he was granted the financial aid. Now the second step was making his way to Bunker Hill Community College to pick out the classes he wanted to take for the fall semester.

"Hey baby, good morning," Baby Fe said, as she walked inside her son's room and gave him a hug and a kiss, "I see the financial aid package came. Did they accept you?"
"Good morning Ma, Yes, they did accept me, and this letter was to let me know that. Now I have to go and pick out some classes for the fall semester."
"That's great baby. I'm so proud of you. Do you have any idea of what classes you want to take?"
"Nah! Not yet. I was thinking about business management or

something in finance. Guess what?"

"What."

"I got my license."

"Congratulations Shyheim, I'm so proud of you." Baby Fe said, as she hugged her son. As she hugged him, she saw a sad look in his eyes and knew something was bothering him. "What's wrong? Why you look like that?"

"Like what?" Scar asked.

"Sad. Why you look sad?"

"You don't want to know." Scar said.

"I wouldn't ask you if I didn't." Baby Fe responded.

Scar broke down and finally said, "Alright, cool. Look, I have been having problems in Boston. I got into a few situations out in the streets."

"Problems with who?"

"A few people."

"What kind of problems are you talking about Shyheim?"

"Minor problems."

"Minor my ass. WHO ARE YOU HAVING PROBLEMS WITH?" Baby Fe shouted.

Scar remained quiet and knew that his mother would have over-reacted if he told her all he had been through since he got out of juvenile detention. "*I can't tell her that I killed that girl, she is going to bug out,*" Scar thought, as he decided to keep his mouth shut.

"Did you call your father and tell him about these problems you are having?"

"Ma! Calm down, calm down. I'm good. I called him, but I didn't tell him what went down. While I was in the project, I ran into an older head named Fresh Eddie, Ma! That nigga said he knows you." Scar said excitedly.

"Who? You must be talking about Eddie Murphy. He's a good nigga. He went to the military straight out of high school and was stationed in Maine and has been there ever since. He's a good friend of your father. That's who your father use to get all his guns from. He owns some type of gun shop up there. He has one of if not the biggest families on the Dark Side. Since you are having problems you need to leave the project alone and focus on your education. Shyheim, I don't want to lose you to these streets. I will call your father and let him know that you are having problems."

"Nah! Ma. I knew I should have had never told you that. It's not that serious. Believe me if it was serious, I would have been called dad."

"Okay. I'm going to take your word. I spoke to your aunt and she said if you wanted you can come to Brookline and live with her."

"I'm cool. I found a safe spot in Allston that no one knows about," Scar said, as he hugged his mother and went to his room. He sat on his bed, took off his hoodie, kicked off his sneakers and laid down and dozed off.

Chapter 26

The next morning Scar heard his mother's footsteps and sat up in bed. He heard her knock lightly and told her to come in. He watched as his mother stepped inside his room fully dressed.

"I'm going to a cook-out and I need you to come. There will be a few people there I would like you to meet."

"What cook-out and who are these people?" Scar asked hesitant.

"My friends. One of them is throwing a cook-out in Lynn. Take a shower and get dressed. We are leaving in an hour."

Scar took a shower, tossed on some black jeans, a black t-shirt, grabbed his .380, and tucked it in his waist. He grabbed his hoodie and walked out of his room.

"Boy, where you think you going in that hoodie and dressed in all black. Its seventy-five degrees out there you better take that hood off and dress appropriately. When you finish grab them two Styrofoam trays and I will meet you outside in the car."

Scar walked back inside the room and found another choice of clothing, grabbed the trays of food and then joined his mother in her SUV. They arrived in Lynn forty minutes later and soon as they pulled up Scar saw a bevy of beautiful females. They stepped out and Scar caught the attention of a thick female with short hair, wire framed glasses and a round face. She stared at Scar as he laid the trays down on the table.

Scar paid her no attention and sat down in a folding chair. She stared at Scar a few more minutes before she had the guts to approach him.

"Hi, what is your name?" The female asked, as she stared at the pear shape scar on Scar's left cheek.

"Terrance." Scar lied.

"My name is Lizzy. Are you from out here in Lynn?"

"No. I'm from the Bean. Do you know where Egleston Square is at?"

"I know where that's at. It's not too far from Academy Homes. How I know is because my sister date a nigga name Free from Academy."

Scar looked at her and wondered why she mentioned Free name and her reasons for approaching him. *"Damn, this might be a set up."* Scar thought, *"nah, my mother wouldn't put me in the line of fire or maybe this bitch talk too much. I need to keep her close."* Scar decided to engage in the conversation and see where it lead. "I just moved to Egleston. I don't know barely anyone.

"The reason why I mentioned my sister boyfriend to you is because he is the man in his hood and if you know him then you might know his friend Bully." Lizzy said shaking her head in disgust. "I don't really like Bully. He always tries to talk to me, but I don't like him. I think that he is ugly and too thirsty."

"I have to play this bitch close to get more information on Free's bitch ass." Scar thought, as he stared at her thick thighs, "I don't know either one of them." Scar knew if he had played his cards right with Lizzy that he could potentially get to Free and kill him and no one would know or have a clue who was behind the killing. "Sit down let's talk. You seem like a cool female to get to know."

The next few hours Scar was listening while Lizzy was talking his ears off. Through her blabber mouth he had learned that she liked to go bowling, roller skating and to go to the movies. He decided to spend as much time as he could with her and hopefully he can gather the information on Free that will lead to his death. After three hours spent at the cook-out it was time to leave. He grabbed a few plates of food and some sodas and followed his mother out of the cook-out.

"I see you met a new friend," Baby Fe said, as they walked to her SUV.
"Yeah! I did. She is a real cool girl. We supposed to go bowling."

"Bowling! Boy, what you know about bowling?"

"Nothing. But I'm going to learn." Scar said seriously, as he opened the passenger door and slid in.

Chapter 27

The weekend after Scar had met Lizzy they agreed to go bowling. So, Scar asked his mother to rent him a car so that he could get around. He drove the rental to Lizzy's house on the Westside of Lynn. He pulled up and beeped the horn. She looked out the window, saw the rental car and came downstairs. She opened the door and got in. She leaned over and gave Scar a kiss on the cheek.

"What street is the bowling alley on?" Scar asked.
"Near the post office. Just drive I will direct the way." Lizzy said.

Lizzy navigated Scar through the city until they reached the bowling alley. Scar parked and waited for Lizzy to step out. He stepped out and joined her in the bowling alley. The next few hours they bowled, played video games and ate snacks. They were having a good time together and all Scar could think about was setting the stage for Free's death. Lizzy drunk a few beers and started to flirt with Scar. He flirted back and started rubbing his hands over her body.

"Come on," Lizzy said.
"Where to?" Scar asked.
"The telly." Lizzy responded.

Scar hesitated and then followed her. He couldn't allow her to choose one so with his quick thoughts he came up with a solution.

"I know a five-star hotel in Boston. You'll love it."
"Okay." Lizzy said.

They pulled up to the Intercontinental hotel near the Boston Aquarium. Scar parked, stepped out, grabbed Lizzy by her waist and walked in the lobby. He paid for the room, stepped on the elevator, and went to the third floor. He slid the pass key in the slot and pushed the door open. He told her to check the room out while he used the bathroom. He stepped inside the bathroom, washed his face and stepped out minutes later. He hung his hoodie on the coat rack and spotted a trail of Lizzy's clothes on the floor. He followed them and looked up and saw her sitting on the bed naked fingering herself. He kicked off his sneakers took off his pants and walked toward her. He didn't have a condom and didn't care if he had one or not. He was only concerned about information about Free.

Lizzy slid back onto the bed and spread her legs. Scar climbed on the bed and was about to enter her raw. "Hold on, let me put this on," Lizzy said, as she rolled the condom on his dick.

Lizzy grabbed Scar's dick and guided it in her pussy. As his dick entered, he started pumping hard and fast shaking the headboard. Lizzy wrapped her arms around Scar's neck as she climaxed two times in a row.

"DAMN, NIGGA BEAT THIS PUSSY UP," Lizzy screamed.

Scar pulled out and lifted Lizzy's legs to his shoulders and started power fucking her with long, hard and deep strokes. The screaming Lizzy gave off was showing that Scar was indeed beating the pussy as she wanted him to do. He flipped her over and started pumping fast and hard in the doggy style position. He came, pulled out and laid beside her on the bed.

"My sister isn't going to believe this!" Lizzy said, as her head rested on Scar's chest.

"How old is your sister?" Scar asked.

"Twenty-two." Lizzy answered.

"That's your older sister?" Scar asked.

"Nah! I'm the oldest."

"What's her name?"

"Sheila."

"She's from out here to?"

"Yeah! But she's always in Boston with her man."

"How long have they been together? You say that like you are jealous."

"They been together for a while. I'm not jealous but she's always with him."

"Enough of them is you ready for round two?" Scar asked.

"Yeah!" Lizzy answered.

Chapter 28

The next thirty days, Scar showed extreme interest in Lizzy. They did a lot of things together in the North Shore. Through her, he learned the best and worst in Lynn. They went out every other night to movies, bowling alleys, skating rinks and even took walks along the Lynn Commons holding hands. All along he was studying Free's routes and set a timetable when he was going to spring his plan into action. In the process of setting his plan of attack Scar rented a rooming house on the next street from Lizzy's house. From his window he could see her front porch.

Instead of driving rentals Scar had decided to use the public transit system because he didn't want to take the chance of his car being spotted in Lynn. He stepped on the train at Back Bay Station with a black book bag. He laid the bag down on the seat and unzipped partially. With the weather starting to change he knew he didn't look out of place with the attire he had on. He was dressed in black jeans, a black army fatigue jacket and some Top Ten Adidas. He had a black ski hat in the bag that doubled over as a ski mask. Scar placed his hand in the bag in case an enemy boarded the train. Six stops later the train rocked gently and pulled to a stop. He looked at the sign Haymarket, took his hand out of the bag, strapped it on his back and walked off the train. He walked outside, saw a taxi stand and made his way towards it. He opened the door to a taxi and slid in.

"Market Square" Scar directed.

The driver nodded and pushed the button for the meter to start. Scar looked out the window as they drove down Lynn Way. They pulled up to Market Square and the driver looked back at Scar and said, "here you go young man".

Scar reached in his pocket, grabbed two twenty-dollar bills and passed it to the driver. He threw the bag over his shoulder and stepped out of the taxi. He walked three blocks before he reached the rooming house that he had rented. He entered the front hallway, climbed the stairs, and stopped at the first door. He used the key to open the door and walked inside. The room came equipped with a bed and a dresser. The only thing he had purchased was a small screen television and an alarm clock. He took off his jacket and placed the bag near the bed. Next, he picked up the alarm clock and set the timer to 7:35pm. He laid down and dozed off.

He woke up a few hours later and saw that it was a quarter till Seven. He stepped out of the bed and walked to the bathroom and stared at the scar on his face. He rubbed the scar with the back of his hand and thought back to the day he had murdered his cousin. He became emotional and walked out of the bathroom and strapped on his vest and grabbed his army fatigue jacket and tossed it on. He grabbed his Mac-10 and placed it in the secret compartment in his jacket and walked out of the house. He walked to the Commons and sat on a bench. Ten minutes later he saw a black Range Rover pull up. He stood up and walked up to the driver side of the Range Rover and pulled out the Mac-10 and pulled the trigger. "BOOM! BOOM! BOOM! BOOM! BOOM! BOOM! BOOM! BOOM! BOOM!"

The thunderous sound of the submachine gun was heard throughout the West End of Lynn. This was when Scar was at his best when he caught his enemies slipping. The lights of the house next door came on, he turned and riddled the side of the house with bullets. He snatched open the door of the Range Rover and squeezed three more shots into Free's lifeless body.

"Closed casket," Scar said, as he ran through the Commons.

Scar went to his pre-arranged spot to stash the guns and change his clothes. After he changed his clothes, he walked past Lizzy's house and saw several police cruisers parked. He smiled threw up the deuces and kept walking to his rooming house.

Chapter 29

Two days after Scar had murdered Free he watched the crime scene
investigators gather evidence, family and friends place flowers and
candles for Free. Scar was to the point where killing became easy to
him. The murders of Free and Wyonna and the shoot-outs made him
desensitize to violence. He looked at it to achieve an end. The formula
for success wasn't any more complicated than meeting violence with
superior violence. After staring out the window for twenty minutes he
turned around and picked up his vest. He looked at all the dents from
when Free had shot him.

*"Damn, I need to go to Maine and holler at Fresh Eddie. I need a
new vest and some more guns."* Scar thought, as he strapped on the
vest.

Scar tossed on his shirt and army fatigue jacket and placed the Beretta in his secret compartment. He hoisted the bag over his shoulder and walked out of the rooming house. He walked past Lizzy's driveway and saw candles and flowers where he had killed Free.

"Have gun will travel," Scar thought.

* * * * * *

Mia was in the process of cooking when she heard the door open. She turned around and saw Scar walking toward her. They hugged and kissed.

"Hey baby," Scar greeted.

"Hey stranger. I haven't seen you in a grip. Where the hell have you been?"

"Out on the west coast with my dad," Scar lied.

"Did you hear that Free from your project got murdered the other day?"

"Yeah! I heard about it. It happened in Revere or something."

"Nah! Lynn." Mia answered.

"Damn, he was good nigga." Scar said.

"I hear he was grimy and murdered a few people. At least that's what the streets say."

"I don't know about all that. Matter fact enough of that. Let him Rest In peace."

"I agree. Are you hungry?" Mia asked.

"Yeah!" Scar said, as he tugged on Mia's shirt, "take that off. What

187

I tell you about shielding them curves. You know I like you cooking naked."

"I know you do, but you have to be here for me to cook naked. I'm not going to cook naked when you aren't here."

"Well, I'm here now so take that shirt off."

Mia cut off the oven burners, lifted her shirt over her head and tossed it on the counter. Scar placed the bag of flower on the floor, zipped down his pants, pulled out his dick and entered her from behind. He grabbed her waist and started pumping hard and fast.

"Damn, this shit is good," he said, as he shot a load of sperm in her. He pulled out, slapped her on the ass cheeks, and backed up.

Mia turned around and got on her knees. Mia had a blow job game that was known city wide as top notch. The streets nicknamed her "Super head", like the video vixen from the way she performed her oral exam. She showed him some of her famous dick sucking tricks. In a matter of minutes he was exploding his protein in her mouth. She swallowed his sperm, got off her knees, washed her hands and saw his extended clip in the window surrounded by plants. He grabbed it and placed it in his back pocket.

"Perfect." Scar thought.

Scar stepped out of the bathroom and walked into the living room. He studied Mia's C.D.'s collection and cursed. "Damn, this bitch has all the Mary J. Blige love shit. I need to listen to some gangster music."

Scar said, as he settled on Tupac "All Eyes on me."

Mia heard "Ambitionz of a Rider" blasting through her sound system and walked into the living room. She placed his plate in front of him and walked toward a recliner. He watched her ass cheeks sway as she walked past him and sat in the recliner. Her thick pussy lips opened as she lifted her left leg on the arm rest. While they ate she watched Scar stare at her pussy. After they finished, she grabbed both plates and walked to the kitchen.

Scar took off the rest of his clothes and walked to the bedroom. He lifted the mattress and saw his .9mm Taurus and picked it up. He extracted the clip and counted each bullet. He placed the gun back under the mattress. Scar lived by morals and standards and in his world, trust had to be earned, and until it was earned, he trusted no one except his parents.

"Mia's a good bitch, but I need someone who is willing to kill for a nigga," Scar thought, as he sat on the bed.

One Arm Abby!

<u>Mi Amor! (My Love)</u>

Next time give me more

than 8 shots.

- One Arm Abby

Cathedral Housing Projects

Chapter 30

Scar laid low for a week after he had murdered Free. He decided it was time to go to the hood and see what the talk is about and who they had suspected of killing Free. He used Mia's car and drove to Dimock Street and parked. He stepped out and walked into the project. He walked to Kia's apartment and knocked on the door. Kia heard the knock, looked through the peep-hole and saw Scar. She opened the door and gave him a hug.

"What's up Scar," she said.
"What's up sis."

Kia stepped to the side and allowed Scar inside the apartment. He walked to the living room and sat down.

"Why you didn't use the key that I gave you?" Kia asked.

"I'm not going to invade your privacy. I wanted to make sure you were home."

"Please remember that you can come here anytime, any day. What me and Pitt do is always behind closed doors. Where you been? I haven't seen you in a while."

"On the low. You know I'm running from the Department of Youth Services."

"I remember you told me that. You heard about your boy Free?"

"Yeah! I saw it on the news."

"Yeah! Whoever killed him riddled him with bullets. His funeral was yesterday and it was a closed casket."

"Damn, that sucks."

"I was just talking about you the other day." Kia said.

"With who?" Scar asked curiously.

"My girl Abby. She wants to meet you."

"What does she look like? Is she pretty?"

"She's pretty. A red bone like Disney. She has long hair, colored eyes, and a nice little body."

"Where did she see me at?"

"She hasn't. I told her about you. She's from Philly and should be here any minute."

"Sis, I'm not pressed to meet new bitches. I'm content with what I already got. Plus, you know I roll solo."

"Believe me she is pretty." Kia assured.

"Alright. I will hear what she has to say. Where's Pitt?"

"Outside. I think he's over on Weaver Way."

"I'm about to check him. Has it been hot around here?" Scar asked.

"Yeah! The gang unit been coming through in that silver car with the tint windows."

"What about Mr. Homicide and the homicide unit?"

"What color car they be in?" Kia asked.

"A blue Crown Victoria." Scar answered.

"Nah! I haven't seen that car since the honor kid got killed."

"Good. I'll be back to see what's up with your girl later," Scar said, as he gave Kia a hug and left.

A couple hours went by and Scar and his crew watched from across the courtyard as a pretty Spanish female knocked on Kia's door.

"Yo! Pitt. Who's that pretty bitch at Kia's door?" Little Barry asked.

"That's some new bitch she met at the welfare office," Pitt said.

"That's the bitch from Philly?" Scar said to himself, as he excused himself and walked to Kia's apartment. He opened the door and walked in the living room and saw Kia and the pretty Spanish female sitting on the couch talking. He stared at the pretty Spanish female. "Damn, she does look good."

Abby looked at Scar and liked what she saw. "*I could work with that.*" She saw the butt of Scar's gun sticking out of his waist and smiled at him.

"Scar, this is my girl Abby."

"Hey, Abby, it's nice to meet you, where are you from?"

"North Philly, the Badlands. I been out here for a little while visiting family."

"Where is your family from?" Scar asked.

"The South end."

"Where at in the South end?"

"Damn, nigga! What you the police asking all these questions," Abby said becoming frustrated with Scar's questioning. "Damn, Kia you didn't say he was going to interrogate me."

"I see you a little feisty Boricua."

"Ain't nothing feisty about me. I'm not use to strangers questioning me soon as they meet me."

"I hear you and understand that cause I don't like being questioned either but are you going to answer the question," Scar said.

"Cathedral Project. What else do you want to know? I wear a size six shoe, I have a thirty-eight C breasts, I don't shave my pussy hair or give a fuck about anyone these days."

"Well, you need to start shaving this isn't the eighteen hundred." Scar said.

"Why? Are you going to do it for me?" Abby smiled.

Scar sat next to Abby, picked up her left hand, examined her nails and the size of her hands. "Do you have a man?"

"No!"

"Why doesn't a pretty girl like you have a man?"

"Because niggas always think they slick. I need a real nigga. Out there in Philly, and here in the Bean, I came across all the wrong niggas."

"You looked in the wrong places when you should have started right here."

"Why would I start here and say you are a real nigga."

"I'm real as they come." Scar said.

"We'll see. Like I said, I need a real nigga. Not a fake one, and when it comes to being that gangster bitch, I'm the one."

"Word," Scar said looking down at her Jordan's, "we don't wear those."

"I know that Adidas is the Boston way of life. I'm on it. Just give a bitch sometime to adjust," Abby snapped with an attitude.

"Only cowards and busters wear Nike's and Jordan's. Real niggas wear Adidas."

"The sneakers a nigga wear don't define realness. I know a lot of fake niggas who wear Adidas and I know real niggas who wear Jordan's and Nike's. I know one thing and that is there is nothing cowardly about me, and nothing new under the sun. I been through a lot and for your information believe me when I say I been there and done that."

"This might be the bitch that I'm looking for," Scar thought, "Come on," he said, "sis we will be back.

"Scar don't get my girl in no shit." Kia said.

"We will be back." Scar said, as he walked out of the apartment followed by Abby. They walked into the woods, down a path to a vacant building.

"So, what's up now, nigga? What you about? Do you get money?" Abby asked, as she eyed Scar's unibrow.

"Yeah! I sell heroin, but I'm on some next shit. If your raggedy ass sticks around, you'll see."

"Raggedy! Nigga, you got me twisted. There is nothing raggedy about

me. I'm the baddest bitch you ever seen! Like I said, what you about?"
"Bitch you talking tough. I want to see how tough you are." Scar said, as he reached in his waist and pulled out a .380 and passed it to her.

Abby didn't blink or show the slightest sign of hesitation when she grabbed the gun. She held it in her left hand, pulled down her sleeve to conceal the gun and looked Scar in the eyes. "This little eight shots isn't nothing."
"Your hands too small." Scar said.
"That's why you use two hands." Abby barked back.
"Oh yeah!" Scar said, as he walked away. He walked toward a log and moved it and reached his hand in the hole. He pulled out a Mac-10 and placed it in his secret compartment in his Army fatigue jacket. He walked back to where Abby was at and pulled out the Mac-10.

Abby's eyes widened at the sight of the Mac-10. "That's what's up nigga. I'm from the Badlands in North Philly and Macs are the guns of choice.
"Follow me" Scar ordered, as he walked out of the woods and toward Bragdon Street.

They walked on Bragdon Street. He stopped and looked at Abby.
"You see them in the courtyard. Put that eighty to use."

Without hesitation Abby walked toward the courtyard. She walked up the stairs and lifted her arm. The Bragdon Street niggas were busy congregating on the benches and never saw Abby approach them. She pulled the trigger. "BOC! BOC! BOC!"

They ducked as bullets whizzed past them. Scar joined her and put the Mac-10 to work. He let off fifteen shots, turned around, and ran back across the street. He ran into the woods and turned to Abby.

Abby took the gun out of her sleeve and handed it to Scar. "Damn, nigga you put every bitch to this test?"
"Nah! You were acting tough, so I wanted to see how tough you were," Scar said, *"damn, I'm bugging if one of them niggas die this bitch might tell. I don't even know this bitch,"* Scar thought, as he looked at Abby, *"but I like the way she moves,"* he thought.
"Next time give me some more shots, and whatever you need me to do, or to be, I'm here for you. I know you don't trust a bitch right now but believe me I'm an asset. Now you seen my gun game, let me see what your dick game is like." Abby said with a smile.

Scar looked at Abby and saw the lust in her eyes and walked out of the woods toward Kia's apartment. Scar used his key to open the door, walked in and cut into Kia son's room. Abby followed him and immediately took off her clothes. Scar saw the curves and liked her even more. He pulled out a condom, took off his pants and stepped toward her.

"Come and give mami some of that big dick." Abby said, licking her lips.

Chapter 31

Scar and Abby finished their two hours of sex and left Kia's apartment. They walked into the courtyard and Abby couldn't help but stare at Scar's handsome features.

"Damn, this is nigga is gangsta. He can fuck and he's cute as hell." Abby thought as she continued to stare at Scar.

Scar saw Abby staring at him from the corner of his eyes. His focus was at the black Mercedes-Benz SL500 that just pulled up into the parking lot. He stood outside of Kia's apartment and saw Cowboy and Trigga emerge from the Mercedes. He looked at Abby and said. "Come on."

Scar walked over to where the older heads were at and gave each of them the three-finger handshake. "What's up Cowboy, what's up Trigga?" Scar greeted as he reached his two favorite niggas from Castlegate. It was Cowboy who had taught Scar a lesson on human anatomy back when he showed him and his cousin Faury the different shapes, and sizes of bullets and how much effect each one had.

"What's up Scar? Damn, you look just like your father." Trigga said. "What's up gee take a walk with me," Cowboy said, as he led Scar to opposite side of the courtyard. "I just found out that Free got killed in Lynn and heard that you had issues with him. Everyone in his circle will assume that you had something to do with it whether you did it or not. I don't know if you know but your father clapped him back in the days. I'm not going to let no-one hurt you but be careful and watch them niggas closely. Them niggas are grimy. Free's younger brother Sincere just came home, pay him close attention he is sneaky. He's not a gunman, but he will pay a nigga to off you."

Scar felt his insides turn to ice, stepped back and rubbed his scar. He knew what he had to do once he came across Sincere. "Good looking out. I'm definitely going to keep an eye on them niggas," Scar said, as he gave dap to Cowboy.

They walked back to where Trigga and the rest of the older heads were at. Scar gave Trigga dap and walked toward Abby, "*I have to go and holler at Fresh Eddie and get another vest and some more guns,*" Scar thought.

Scar reached Abby and stared at her. She saw the crazed look in his eyes and wondered what him and Cowboy had spoken about and what was next. "I have some business to attend to out of state. I need you to come with me." Scar said.

"No problem. Where are we going?" Abby asked.

"Maine. I need to visit a good friend of mines. I'm going to go home and clean myself up and then I will meet you at South Station tomorrow morning."

"Alright. Call me when you ready."

"I got you." Scar said, as he hugged and kissed Abby, "do you need me to drop you off?"

"Nah! I have wheels." Abby answered.

Scar walked toward Mia's car and slid in. He thought about what Cowboy had told him. He knew his beef with the older heads from his project was far from over. He put the car in drive and drove to Mia's house. He pulled up and parked outside and sat in the car. He pulled out his phone and called Fresh Eddie. He told Fresh Eddie that he needed to see him.

Scar finished the call and then stepped inside the house. He went straight into the room and reached under the bed. He pulled out a blue Adidas box and opened it. He pulled out a few stacks of money and counted five thousand dollars. He put the money to the side and slid the box back under the bed. When he turned around, he saw Mia walking inside the room.

"Hi! Baby," Mia said, as she kissed Scar.

"What's up baby? I am about to take this road trip tomorrow to handle some business. I will be gone for a few days."

"Where are you going?"

"New Hampshire." Scar lied.

"O.k. While you are gone is there anything that you would like me to do?"

"Nah! If something comes up then I will let you know" Scar said, as he wondered if Slice would be finished with the bricks of heroin he had left him. "I had a long day today and about to lay it down." He said, as he grabbed Mia by the waist and held her close, "take off these clothes."

Mia took off her clothes and joined Scar on the bed. Scar rubbed Mia's body and rubbed his fingers over her pussy lips and then inserted one inside and started pleasuring her. Mia moaned as his finger dipped in and out of her pussy.

"Take off your clothes," Mia said.

Scar obliged by her demand and took off his clothes. He grabbed Mia by her ankles and spread her legs. He aimed his dick at her opening and started stroking. The next hour they sexed each other and then fell asleep in each other's arms.

Chapter 32

The next morning Scar woke up and called Abby. He told her he was on the move. Mia drove him to the bus terminal and gave him a kiss before he stepped out. He walked to the entrance of South Station Bus Terminal and took the escalator upstairs. He saw Abby sitting on a bench reading a Guns & Ammo Magazine. Abby looked up and saw Scar coming her way. She folded the magazine, laid it on the bench and stood up.

"Hi baby, I see you made it," Scar said, as he stared at Abby, "how long you been here?"

"Twenty minutes," Abby said, as she passed Scar his bus ticket, "the bus leaves in twenty minutes."

"Thanks. I'm glad that you are able to make the trip with me."
Scar said.

"I will always be there when you need me," Abby said.

Scar explained to Abby his purpose for the trip to Maine and how he needed her to leave a few days earlier with a few of his guns. They saw people forming a line and stepped up.

"Let's get in line now, so we can get a good seat." Scar said.
Abby and Scar stepped onto the bus and found two empty seats in the middle row. Abby reached in her purse and pulled out her magazine and started reading about a .9mm made by the Israeli Military Industry called the Jericho.

The whole ride to Maine Abby read the Guns & Ammo Magazine. The bus pulled up to the Greyhound Bus Terminal in Portland, Maine. They stepped off and Scar reached in his pocket, pulled out a piece of paper and followed the directions to Fresh Eddie's house. They walked down St. John Street. Scar followed the directions that Fresh Eddie gave him. They took a left on Valley Street and then a quick right on A-Street. Scar found Fresh Eddie's house and knocked on the door.

Fresh Eddie opened the door and saw Scar and a pretty Spanish female. "What's up Scar?"

"What's up Eddie? This is my girl Abby."

"What's up Abby. It's nice to meet you," he said, as he stepped to the side and allowed them in.

Scar and Abby walked in and followed Fresh Eddie to the living room. Scar saw how clean the house was. *"Damn, this spot is nice,"* Scar thought as he looked at all the nice furnishings.

"What can I help you with?" Fresh Eddie asked, as he sat on a sofa.

"I need some handguns and a couple bullet proof vests."

"What kind of guns?" Fresh Eddie asked.

"Any kind except Brycos, Davidsons and Hi-points." Scar answered.

"And don't forget about Jennings. Those shits are trash." Abby chimed in, "can you get this? Abby asked, as she passed Fresh Eddie the magazine.

Fresh Eddie grabbed the magazine and saw a picture of a gun called the Jericho. He read about it and looked at Abby.

"I know what this is. This is what you want?" He asked, as he explained to Abby about the Israeli handgun.

"Yeah! This is what we are looking for." Abby answered.

"Alright. Anything else you want?" Fresh Eddie asked.

"What about Heckler and Koch's Handguns?" Abby asked.

"I can get my hands on those. How many are you talking?" Fresh Eddie asked.

"Well, what can I get for five thousand dollars?" Scar asked.

"Five thou, I can get you two Jericho's, a Heckler and Koch .45 and a level four Kevlar Vest. Do any of y'all have a criminal record?"

"I do." Scar answered, "I got that smack from when I was twelve."

"You should be good since you were a juvey." Fresh Eddie said.

"Damn, nigga you clipped someone at twelve?" Abby asked.

"Yeah! It's a long story."

"You didn't get bound over or nothing?" Fresh Eddie asked.

"Nah! I was committed to DYS until my Twenty-first birthday and since I been home I been on AWOL status." Scar said.

"I don't want to chance it. What about you Abby?" Fresh Eddie asked.

"I'll do it. My record is as clean as a whistle."

"Alright this is the deal. As you know I own a gun shop up here and what I can do is put your order legally, but a week or so after you buy the guns report them stolen. The guns will already have the serial numbers obliterated. All that is required is a background check and some papers to be filed to the ATF. It should take about a week to get the order, but in the meantime, Abby I need you to get a Maine State I.D."

"That's no problem." Abby said.

"If you want y'all can stay here."

"Nah! We cool enjoy your privacy. Me and my girl is going to check into a hotel. What's a good hotel around here?"

"You got the Inn at St. John over on Congress Street, It's right across the street from the bus terminal."

"Word. I didn't see no hotel. Since it's close by that would do. I'm hungry as hell. What's up with Pizza Villa? I heard a few people on the bus talking about it."

"Nah! Stay away from there that's the D.E.A. hang-out. Whatever you have a taste for you can find it around here."

"I got a taste for some Chinese food. Where's the Chinese food spots at?"

"Down the street is Langs Express. They got some banging chicken lo-Mein."

"I'm going to check it out, do you want anything?"

"Nah! I'm straight. A week from today stop by the gun shop and your order should be ready. The shop is on Congress Street. You can't miss it, out front is a big sign that reads 'Pine Tree Armory'."

"We'll be there." Scar said, as he gave Fresh Eddie a pound and a hug.

"I'm about to see what's up with this telly and tomorrow me and Abby will get on that I.D. thing."

Make sure you do. It's needed to put in the order for the guns."

"It was nice meeting you" Abby said, as she stood up and gave Fresh Eddie a hug and followed Scar out of the front door.

Chapter 33

Young Josh was an up-and-coming hustler from Codman Park on the Light Side of Academy Homes. He hustled the graveyard shift and it served him well. The past five days treated the young hustler good. He flipped sixty-two grams each day, except today. Today he sold 120 grams, all in a matter of seven hours and with five more grams to go he would have set a milestone in his young career. When Lawsons opened up he was usually the first one in the chair to get his weekly haircut. He looked at his watch and saw that it was 8:30am. He looked and saw Tanya opening up the shop. He waited ten minutes before he entered.

"What's up Tanya," Young Josh said, as he walked into the shop, took off his cap and sat in her chair.

Twenty minutes later Tanya released the neck strip and pulled off the cape. She passed the young hustler the mirror. He looked at his fresh spinning waves and passed her back the mirror.

"That's right," Young Josh said, admiring his wavy hair.
Young Josh was a light skin, pudgy face hustler who idolized the older hustlers in his project and dreamed of one day being just like them. He reached in his pocket and pulled out a knot of twenties, peeled one off and slid it to Tanya. "Keep the change," he said, as he grabbed his one size too big yellow Oakland Athletic baseball cap and tossed it on his head. He walked outside of the barbershop and saw his man Pump walking down the street. Being the only one with crack this early served Young Josh well; he learned that getting money from 1am to

211

8am was the best hours to hustle. "Let me get three," a crack head said holding up a fifty-dollar bill.

Young Josh spit out three rocks from his mouth and passed them to the crackhead. "Here you go." He said.

Young Josh took the money and stuffed it in his green Champion sweatpants. Another crackhead walked up to the chubby hustler.

"Six for a hundred." Another crack head said.
"I only have five, but give me eighty," Young Josh said, taking the money. "It's rocking out here. I'm about to go home, get some rest and then call Bully and get some more coke."
"Damn, Josh you look right. That A's jacket is you. What's that Mitchell and Ness?" Pump asked walking over to Young Josh.
"Yeah! This is that vintage nineteen-seventy-two throw-back limited-edition shit."

Young Josh knew he was fresh and didn't have to be reminded. He was a true-blue Light Side nigga. He pulled out a rolled blunt and smoked it with Pump. After they finished smoking, he gave dap to Pump and turned his baseball cap backwards. He grabbed a mountain bike from the wall, jumped on it, and told Pump he would be back.

* * * * * *

Blammer pulled up and parked outside of his cousin Cuckoo's house on Walnut Street. He reached under his seat and pulled out his .357 and placed it in his waist. He opened the door and stepped out. He walked to the building and rang the doorbell. Cuckoo looked out the window and saw his cousin Blammer. He buzzed the door and waited for Blammer to join him in the apartment.

"What's up cuz?" Blammer said, as he gave his cousin dap and walked inside the house.

"What's up dawg. It's almost nine o'clock what brings you here this early?"

"I just left this bitch crib and wanted to see what's up with you. I have a lot on my mind and you my dawg, so I know that you would understand if no one else will."

"What's on your mind? Talk to me cuz."

"I'm out here going hard putting niggas to sleep, filling niggas with holes and getting into wild wild west shoot-outs. My father just came home, and we spoke about a few things and he wants me to pursue this music thing. Music is my passion, but I love this street shit too and I got my eyes on this nigga from the A."

"I never knew Academy and the Point had beef."

"We don't. Do you remember back in the days when my older brother Faury got killed?"

"Yeah!"

"Well the nigga who was locked up for it is out. I ran into him at the D.R.C. and I wanted to hear his side of the story and then some nigga name Murder walked up. When I was speaking to the nigga about what happened and got fly with me, pulled out a gun but didn't use it.

I was pissed and left. Then I caught up with the nigga who killed my brother at the Vous and he told me what happened the day my brother got killed. While we were talking he told me that he had the nigga Murder's back. So, you know me, I went to get at the nigga Murder the next day and ended up getting in a toot out with the nigga from Academy."

"Sounds like some personal shit to me. You know cuz once you bring it to a hood over personal issues then a lot of people could get hurt. Be careful them Academy niggas have a team of killers on their team."

"So do we. You talking like the Point is soft or something."

"I am not saying that. All I'm saying is if you want to keep it personal or go to war. What's the nigga from Academy name?"

"Scar. Do you know him?"

"Nah! But I been hearing his name. So, what's on your mind?" Cuckoo asked.

"You already know," Blammer said with a smile. "I'm in war mode."

"I'm not fucking with you. Last time we collaborated a few years back we fucked around and killed that innocent kid."

"Yeah! That was fucked up. I still have nightmares about that one, but what is done is done." Blammer said.

Cuckoo agreed with his cousin. "Let's go down Dudley and get something to eat. You never know we might catch one of the O.P. niggas slipping." They walked out of the apartment and to Blammer's car.

"Take the wheel," Blammer said, as he tossed his cousin the keys.

Cuckoo caught the keys and opened the driver's door. They slid in and pulled off. Blammer pulled out his .357 and put it on his lap.

Young Josh was riding up Washington Street on a yellow Cannondale Mountain Bike. He knew he was killing them with his oversized baseball cap, matching jacket, Champion sweatpants, and his green and yellow patent leather Adidas. He was high from the weed he had smoked with Pump.

"Yo! Blammer. "Cuckoo said, as he spotted a nigga with an Oakland Athletics cap on.
"Hold on cuz, let me get busy," Blammer said, as he grabbed his gun from his lap.
Cuckoo pulled up to Young Josh and hit the brakes. Blammer leaned his body out of the car window and pointed the .357 at Young Josh's head.

Young Josh was so deep in thought about making money that he didn't see the gun pointed at him.

"TIMES UP!" Blammer yelled and pulled the trigger. "BOOM! BOOM! BOOM!"

The Hollow tip bullets flew out of the .357 and crashed into Young Josh's head. His Oakland Athletics Cap, brain fragments and blood decorated the brick wall. He was dead before he hit the ground. Blammer stepped out, lowered his gun, and shot Young Josh two more times. He walked back to the car, bowed and shouted. "CAN SOMEBODY CALL THE CORONER. THIS NIGGA IS DEAD!"

Chapter 34

The next week Scar and Abby walked in Pine Tree Armory and headed straight to the back. On their way to the back Scar saw that several racks were filled with holsters, goggles, magazines, speed loaders, range bags, cleaning solutions and paper targets. Fresh Eddie stood behind a waist high display case that had several Smith & Wesson, Colts, Glocks, and Sig Sauers. He saw Abby and Scar walking toward him and smiled.

"What's up bro," Scar said, as he gave Fresh Eddie the Threes. "This joint is nice how you come up with this?" Scar asked, as he looked around the shop.

"After I came from the Navy, I saw there was an opportunity to make some money from pushing hammers and I looked into what was needed to open up a business. I obtained my F.F.L. and me and one of my Navy Seal brothers opened this joint up. I had this joint for close to fifteen years now. A few years back I bought out my partner and now I own one hundred percent of the business."

"What kind of license do you need to operate one of these?"

"It's called an F.F.L. That's short for Federal Firearms License."

"That's good shit. Did the order come in yet?"

"Yeah! Hold on," Fresh Eddie said, as he walked to the back. A couple minutes later he came out with a bag and placed it on the display case. He zipped it open and pulled out the twin Jericho's, the Heckler and Koch 45."

"Damn, these are some pretty Tones," Scar said, as he stared at the guns. He picked up the Heckler & Koch and kissed it. "This is going to be glued to my hip." Scar said, as he admired how pretty the gun was.

"Abby were you able to obtain the Maine State I.D.?"

"Yeah!" Abby said, as she reached in her purse, pulled out the I.D. and passed it to Fresh Eddie.

Fresh Eddie grabbed her I.D. and disappeared. He came back a minute later and passed her an ATF form. "I need you to fill out this form."

"What's this?" Abby asked.

"It's an ATF form 4473. Be honest when filling it out because if you lie on the format it will result in you being charged with a felony. Let me put these hammers in the bag for you," Fresh Eddie said, as he grabbed the .45 from Scar. "Remember that the serial numbers is obliterated and don't forget to report these stolen a week from today."

"Got you." Scar said.

After Abby finished filling out the form, she passed it to Fresh Eddie. He grabbed it and walked to a phone. Abby and Scar waited for twenty minutes until the FBI called Fresh Eddie and told him to proceed with the order.

"Abby, I put a little gift in there for you as well." Fresh Eddie said, as he reached in the bag and pulled out a six shot Glock 43 pistol. "This is yours."

"Thanks." Abby said, as she stared at the gun with a smile on her face. "What's the bus schedule?" Abby asked.

"The best bus to take is the Concord Trailways. It's a safer route because it's a non-stop trip. The bus leaves every hour."

"I'm going to meet you back in the hood tomorrow. I'm going to spend the rest of the day up here. I don't want to bring any extra attention to you." Scar said.

"Alright baby, I understand. I'm going to take a taxi to the bus terminal and head home. I will see you tomorrow." Abby said, as she gave Scar a hug and a kiss.

"Be safe and I'll see you when I come home."

"I will. Thanks Eddie. We appreciate what you did for us."

"No problem y'all family. Abby there is a taxi stand right across the street and remember the name of the bus terminal is Concord Trailways."

"Ok." Abby said.

"Call me when you get home." Scar said.

"I will." Abby said, as she walked out of the Armory.

Scar spent the next few hours with Fresh Eddie until he closed the shop for the night. They went out to dinner at the Old Port and then headed to the strip club in South Portland. After the strip club they brought a few strippers to a hotel and tag teamed them. After they left the hotel Scar fell asleep on Fresh Eddies couch. In the morning he woke up, strapped on the bullet-proof vest and put the shoulder holsters in the bag and then left.

It took Scar less than 2 hours to reach Boston from Portland, Maine. He stepped off the bus and took a taxi to Abby's apartment in Cathedral Housing Project. Abby was sitting on the stairs with a Puerto Rican guy with long braids when the taxi pulled up.

"Who the fuck is she with?" Scar said, as he saw Abby on the stairs of her apartment building. He paid the fare and stepped out of the taxi.

Abby got up from the stairs and ran over to Scar and gave him a big hug and a kiss on his lips. She grabbed his hand and walked him over to the stairs where her Puerto-Rican friend was sitting. "I want you to meet my friend Jose."
"Jose. Who is that?"
"He's the man to see. I told him about you, and he wants to meet you. Don't worry he is cool I know his family. He's project born and a real good hustler."
"What he's looking for work?"

"Yeah!"

"Well, put him on."

They made it over to Jose and Abby introduced Scar to Jose and invited him into her house so that they could talk. Once inside the apartment they spoke for twenty minutes about loyalty and trust. Scar made it known to Jose that he would hustle for Abby and her only. He agreed and left the apartment.

Scar watched from the window as Jose exited the apartment building and walked across the courtyard. He turned around and joined Abby inside the bedroom. He saw the duffel bag and opened it. He pulled the Jericho and the Heckler & Koch out of the bag and placed them on the dresser.

"Where's the other Jericho?" Scar asked.

"On the hip where it belongs." Abby answered.

"I see you keeping that bad boy close to you." Scar said with a smile on his face.

"It's already part of my physique," Abby said, as she pulled up her shirt showing him the gun.

Scar picked up the other Jericho, studied it and looked at Abby. He

gave her a thumbs up for selecting a good weapon of mass destruction.

"I'm going to give this bad boy to Pitt," Scar said, as he grabbed the Heckler & Koch, "take me to Kia's apartment."

Abby grabbed a sweater and tossed it on. She opened the doors and they walked out of the apartment. "Do you want to drive?" Abby asked.

"Nah! I'm good."

Abby drove to Academy Homes and parked outside of Kia's apartment. Scar noticed that the parking lot was empty and knew that the police had cleared the block. They got out of the car and Scar used his key to enter the apartment. They walked into the living room and saw Pitt and Kia watching T.V. He walked over to Kia and gave her a kiss and a hug and introduced Pitt to Abby.

"Bro, let me talk to you for a minute." Scar said, as he pulled Pitt to the side. They walked a few feet away and Scar reached in his pants and pulled out the gun and passed it to Pitt. "This is yours?" Scar said. "Good look," Pitt said, as he examined the Heckler & Koch. "It's hot as hell out here. The young nigga Josh from the Light Side got murdered a few days back and the homicide unit and every other unit been lurking around here. That's the third murder around here in the past couple months. The chump "Mr. Homicide" been threatening niggas; if no one gets arrested for the honor student he will start framing niggas for bodies. I just been chilling indoors and laying low, that cracker is crazy. That little bitch you got is a winner dawg, I know she got that snapper?"

"You know she does dawg," Scar laughed, "She's a rider, hustler and a nympho." Scar said, as he thought about what Pitt had said about how hot the project was. "I'm going to stay away from here. I can't chance getting picked up on some small shit and spending the next couple years in D.Y.S.. I must move discreetly because I can't afford to get caught slipping or bagged. I'm doing too good out here dawg. I still got that spot in St. Joes but since I almost got shot on my way there I kind of fell back from there. I think I'm going to open shop in Cathedral with Abby."

"I hear that. This shit is like a desert around here. I never saw so many police swing through here in my life. Oh Yeah dawg, the nigga Bully's brother Sincere is home. "He hadn't come around here yet, but when he came to his brother's funeral, he had asked a few people about you. I guess the nigga is laying low.

"Fuck them niggas. I'm not going to let a nigga catch me slipping again. They caught me once, but not again," Scar said, as he thought about how he had killed Free in Lynn. "What's up with Sincere? What kind of nigga is he?"

"A master manipulator." Pitt informed, "but one thing I can say is that he is about making that paper, but he is known to manipulate others to do his dirty work."

"Good look. I just stopped by to drop that hammer off to you. That thing right there," Scar said referring to the Heckler & Koch "is a game changer."

"Thanks. I appreciate you dawg."

"Anytime." Scar said giving Pitt dap before him and Abby left the apartment.

Chapter 35

Sincere was what you called an O.G. He ran in the same circle as the Academy legends: D-Square and Spaine. He used his O.G. status to his advantage as he out hustled his peers and flooded the project with cocaine. He was a natural hustler who knew how to stack, invest, and spend his money wisely. Besides Uncle Stretch, Sincere was the best hustler to ever do it in Academy Homes.

Sincere was in a medium security prison in Gardiner, Massachusetts when he received the news that his older brother Free had been murdered. The murder made him angry. He was pissed because he kept hearing that a little nigga named Scar might of have been the one responsible and it seemed like no one attempted to exact revenge. Sincere been home for a couple weeks and the first thing he had done when he stepped out of prison was taken a trip down to Atlanta. His family from Atlanta blessed him with five kilos of cocaine. He took the kilos to Archdale and Beech Street housing projects in Roslindale and made an easy hundred thousand.

Sincere decided to make his rounds in the project and the first stop was to the Dark Side. He walked down Weaver Way and saw a group standing near a Mercedes-Benz. Across the courtyard five men stood by the trunk of Riot's Mercedes-Benz smoking blunts. Riot and Little Barry had handguns tucked in their waists, Pitt had a snub nose .357 sticking out his pocket and Curly had a .38 Special in his hand. Sincere recognized Scar leaning on a railing. It took great effort on his part to conceal his hatred for the nigga who was told might be responsible for his brother's death. He watched Scar closely and walked over toward his crew.

"Yo! What's up Sin," Little Barry said, as he gave him dap, "welcome home."
"Thanks. I see everyone looking like new money out here. I like to see my niggas getting money," Sincere said, as he gave dap to each Wolf Pack member. "What's up Scar?" He said, as he gave Scar dap.

This was Scar's first time seeing Sincere and was glad that he could finally put a face with the name.

"What's up Sin? It's finally nice to meet the man I hear so much about." Scar said.

"Likewise. How's your moms doing?"

"She's good." Scar answered.

"Tell her and your dad I said what's up."

"No doubt. I will tell both of them that you send your regards."

"Yo! Pitt. What's up with this show I keep hearing about?" Sincere asked.

"What, the show we supposed to throw with them Franklin Hill and Castlegate niggas?"

"Yeah! I guess. I hear it's supposed to be big."

"Yeah! It's going to be nice." Pitt said.

"You know before I went in, I was the brain behind ATH Promotions, it's nothing for me to reach out and see if I can get an A list rapper or something to come and perform or do a walk through."

"It's not up to me. You have to talk to Trigga, Nice and White Boy Bink they are the ones who are sponsoring the show." Pitt said.

"I'll holler at them niggas and see what I can contribute. I'm about to head to the other side." Sincere said, as he gave everyone a pound and a hug. He knew that he would have to check up on Scar to put the truth to the rumors and if the Wolf Pack joined Scar then it would be a murder show. As he walked to the Light Side he thought about the essence of Free and Uncle Stretch's beef.

Twelve years back, Free grabbed a handful of Baby Fe's butt. She turned around, slapped him and shouted death threats. Free spit a lungi in Baby Fe's face and called her all types of names and dared her to do something. She did do something; called Uncle Stretch. He rode up on a motorcycle, beat Free, and warned him the next time would be his death. It was Sincere who had squashed the beef between the two. After Sincere got locked Free had words with Uncle Stretch and ended up getting shot three times.

Sincere walked over to the Light Side and approached a crowd that huddled inside one of the project hallways. All the top dogs were there playing dice. Sincere never played dice in a project hallway, outside, in an alley or anywhere. Playing dice was a no-no after his man Mike Love was murdered at a dice game. He couldn't fathom why someone would be willing to lose money instead of gaining it. He walked over to Bully and Tomb and gave them dap.

"When is the nigga Young Josh's funeral?" Sincere asked.
"In a couple days." Bully answered.
"Make sure you give his mother a couple racks." Sincere said.
"Alright."
"Did niggas rectify the situation?"
"Not yet!" Bully said.
"Why not? Who was responsible?" Sincere asked.
"Niggas not sure who did it. I think it was them Bragdon niggas. A few days before he was killed a few niggas got hit up on Bragdon."
"Oh! Alright. Be safe out here. What's up with this little nigga?" Sincere asked, as he pointed to Rabbit.
"He rolls with them Wolf Pack niggas." Bully said.
"Oh yeah! That's not being a true-blue Light Side nigga. Who's his family these days?"
"It's just him and his little sister." Bully informed.

"How old is she?" Sincere asked.

"Young. She goes to the Ellis school."

"Well let's see how deep his loyalty is. For the next two weeks follow the little girl to and from school. Time all her movements and then snatch her one day after school. We going to use this nigga to do our dirty work," Sincere said, as he gave Bully dap.

"You trust that nigga?" Bully asked, referring to Rabbit.

"Does he love his sister?" Sincere asked with a smile.

"Nuff said," Bully said, as he looked at Rabbit with a smile.

* * * * * *

As Sincere and his crew was plotting on Scar's demise, Scar on the Other hand was in deep thought about all the murders that were happening and started to become paranoid. He had no idea who had killed Young Josh and was beginning to think that it was the Point because of where he had gotten killed at. He decided to lay low from hustling in St. Joe's and decided to give Jose some heroin to sell. He tested him out with a couple bundles and then a few days later he gave him a couple of bricks. A bundle is ten bags and bricks are five bundles. Jose proved each time he was about his money.

Scar sat on the bench next to Abby reading a newspaper. He folded the paper and placed it on the bench. Abby stepped up, looked at Scar and walked away. Scar followed her to the other side of the housing project. They walked past a pole that had a flyer attached to it. Scar stopped and read the flyer.

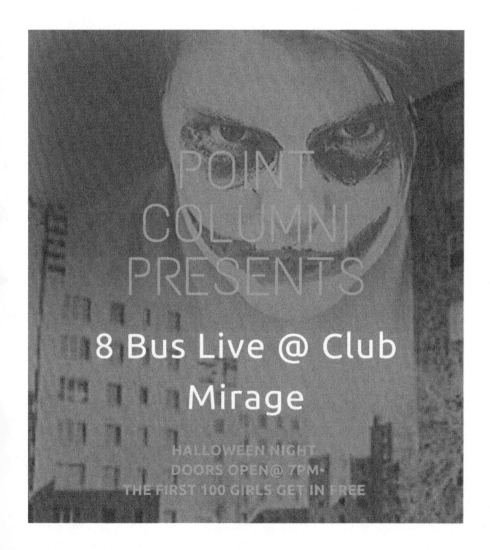

"Damn, it's just that easy," Scar thought, thinking that this was where he would finish Blammer. "I'm going to spend Halloween with my

grandmother and then I'll call you when I get there." Scar said, as he kissed Abby.

"Okay. Be safe and make sure you call me."

"I will." Scar said, as he walked away.

Chapter 36

Scar spent the next couple days at his mother's house and then he followed his mother in his rental to his grandmother's house to help pass out the candy to the children in the neighborhood for Halloween. This was Scar's first time celebrating any holiday with his family in five years. He took this time to sit down and talk to his Aunt Tay about her life and how he was proud of her for all the stuff she was doing with her stop the violence movement. He apologized to her for what happened the day Faury was shot and killed. Scar's apologies brought back memories to the day she learned of her son's death from the doctor. That was the worst time of her life when Faury died because a few months later her oldest son Ramel was arrested for over 100 grams of cocaine and sentenced to serve 10 years in a federal prison. "How is Ramel doing?" Scar asked.

"Good. They moved him to a prison in Otisville, New York."

"Tell him. I said what's up and that I miss and love him."

"You should write him and Quamie. They would love to hear from you. I will tell him that you said what's up. How are you? Your mother told me you are running these streets like a chicken with your head cut off. Be careful out here Shyheim, these streets don't love anyone."

"I'm not running wild out here. I am making advances in my life while still trying to survive. I will be okay auntie believe me I can hold my ow. How are you and what you been up to lately?"

"Just working and keeping my sanity. You know I been traveling all over the country for the past five years. They offered me a job in Washington D.C. to help set up a similar movement. I politely declined because I'm not doing this for money. I'm doing this cause my heart is into it and I want to see all the negativity turn into positivity. These kids don't even know why they are killing each other. I remember when I was young my brother told me that they were beefing with Humbouldt over a bike and a girl."

"Are you serious?"

"Yes. I am and look how many people lost their lives over something so senseless. I can't wait till Quamie comes home in the spring. I will have a long talk with him because it seems to me that he is still caught up in this street life. You should see him he has gotten big over the years. He looks like a giant in there."

"I know. My mother showed me a picture of him. I almost didn't recognize him." Scar said. "When you get a chance slide me their addresses. I want to write to them and send them some money and pictures."

Tay wrote down their addresses and gave them to Scar. "Please write to them. They would love to hear from you Shyheim and please think twice before you do anything in these streets. You spent too much of your young life already and don't need to waste anymore over frivolous behavior."

After he finished talking to his aunt, he dedicated the next couple hours passing out candy to the kids in the neighborhood with his family. He gave his grandmother, mother and his aunt hugs and kisses and then left. He walked to his rental car, opened the door and slid into the driver's seat. He looked at his watch and saw that it was close to 9:30pm. "Perfect timing," Scar said, as he put the car in drive and pulled off.

Scar made it to the city and drove straight to Abby's house. He parked outside her building and saw the project was empty. He stepped out of the car and walked inside the building. He walked up the stairs and used his key to open the door. Abby was sitting in the living room reading the Guns & Ammo Magazine when Scar walked in. She saw that Scar had a smile on his face and placed the magazine down on the coffee table and walked over and gave him a hug. They spoke for fifteen minutes.

"I'll be back. I need to go and holler at Slice down the Joe's and see what's up with him." Scar said, as he kissed Abby on the lips and walked toward the door.

"Don't be too long. You know what today is." Abby said.

"I know. Just get dressed. I will be back." Scar replied.

Scar decided to drive past Club Mirage to see if he could spot Blammer. He walked out of the building and to his car. He slid in the driver's seat, pulled out his gun and placed it on his lap. He put the car in drive and pulled off.

* * * * * *

Nastee was putting the final touches on the show. He hired a photographer to snap photos and a videographer to tape the show. He wanted this show to be a memorable one. He walked around the club and inspected every area and made sure that no weapons were stashed. He was proud that his son decided to take his rap career serious.

"I'm going to push my little man to stardom. This event is going to be a smash," Nastee thought.

Scar drove past Club Mirage and saw dozens of Columbia Point niggas standing out front in leather coats and Philadelphia Phillies and Pittsburgh Pirates caps. He wanted to park, hop out, and fire into the crowd but logically thinking he would have not made it out alive because with the dozens of niggas standing there, he figured half of them would be strapped and it would be suicide.

Chapter 37

Blammer stood outside of the club talking to a few members of his gang. He was still riding high off the murder of Young Josh. In his eyes he believed he was winning the war against Scar and his crew. He was proud of everything he had achieved in the streets; especially his murderous reputation. A few minutes later he marched inside the club with his crew. He saw two pretty Spanish females near the bar and invited them to the V.I.P. Section. Nastee was in the V.I.P. section talking to Terrible Trav when he saw his son walk in with two pretty Spanish females. He excused himself and went over and pulled his son to the side.

"You ready to put Boston on the map?" Nastee asked.
"Yeah! I'm ready. Thanks, dad, for making this happen. It feels like a

dream but looking at all the people who came to show love makes me know that it's real.

"I see you got nice taste in women" Nastee said, as he nodded to the two Spanish females."

"These bitches are groupies so I'm going to treat them as groupies"

"I hear that."

"I'm about to get ready and do these tracks" Blammer said, as he hugged his father and walked out of the V.I.P. section.

Nastee watched from the V.I.P. section as his son and his crew performed a few of their tracks.

"Damn, these little niggas got skills," Nastee said, as he saw a Brazilian female staring at him.

Nastee walked over to her and introduced himself. "Hi! My name is Byron. What's your name?"

"Gloria, but everyone calls me Glo."

"Well, are you enjoying yourself tonight Glo?"

"Yes. I like this. I'm visiting the area and heard about this show and decided to come out tonight and enjoy myself."

"I'm glad to see that you're enjoying the night. What are you doing after the show?"

"Nothing. Why what you have planned?"

"If you want, me and you can slide and get to know each other on a different level." Nastee smiled.

"We can do that, but I can't leave my girls here. We came together and planned to leave together."

"I have a solution for that. Most of my niggas are here," Nastee said, as he pointed to the V.I.P. area, "if your girls see someone they like then we all can go out and enjoy dinner."

"That sounds good. Let me talk to my girls and I will be back to talk to you more."

"Matter fact, why don't you and your girls step up in the V.I.P. area and enjoy yourself in luxury."

"Okay." Gloria said, as she laughed.

After Blammer finished his performance Nastee, Terrible Trav and a couple others left the club and went out to eat with Gloria and her friends.

* * * * * *

Two blocks down from Club Mirage a homeless woman shuffled down the street singing church songs in a dirty white coat that was three sizes too big for her frame. Her light skin was covered with dirt, her hair stuck out from underneath her tan scarf as she roamed the street pushing a metal shopping carriage collecting bottles. Her eyes were alert, her posture slouched, and demeanor erratic. She saw the crowd outside the club and kept forward.

Abby played the role of the bum. She learned this method of assassination from reading about old school gangsters. She knew what she was about to do was a suicide mission but figured with her disguise she could pull it off.

The two Spanish females were now pissy drunk and rubbing all over Blammer's chest. He grabbed the two and walked outside and straight to his BMW. He looked down the street and saw a homeless woman pushing a carriage walking his way. He opened the door and slid in the passenger seat.

Abby was a few feet away from Venom's BMW and without hesitation raised her left arm and pulled the trigger. The bullets flew out of her sleeve and crashed into Blammer's head as he sat in the passenger seat. The sound of gunfire caused the two Spanish females to scream and jump out of the car.

"*Never fails*," Abby thought, as she pushed the carriage away and blew a few shots at the other niggas.

Abby ran toward her car when two shots whizzed past her. She spun around and blew two more shots in their direction. She made it to the car, hopped in and exhaled.

Scar drove Abby's car down Tremont Street, took a turn on Washington Street and headed toward Cathedral project. He pulled up inside the housing project and stopped outside of Abby's building. They stepped out, he hugged and kissed her and said. "You get cleaned up and I'm going to go stash these guns and switch cars." Scar said, as he grabbed the Glock 43 from Abby.

Scar watched her open the hallway door and walk inside the building. He walked to his car, opened the door and slid in. He put the car in drive and drove out of the project.

Chapter 38

Nastee was at Chow-Chow's when he got the call that his son was shot. He leaned over and whispered what happened in Terrible Trav's ear and paid for the meal and excused himself from Gloria and her friends.

"Come on dawg, we are going to the hospital," Nastee said, as he trotted to his car.

They got in the car and Nastee sped off. He drove to Boston Medical Center and saw a few females standing outside of the emergency exit crying. He stormed past them and walked inside the hospital. The first person he saw was his son's right-hand man "Venom".

"Yo! Venom what the fuck happened to my son?" Nastee asked hysterically. "How the fuck this happen?"

"He was in his BMW ready to leave and someone came up on him dressed like a bum and shot him."

"Where did he get shot? Is he okay, where's the doctors and nurses?" Nastee asked, as he began to panic.

"In the face and neck. It doesn't look good." Venom answered.

Nastee grabbed a chair and flipped it over. The hospital security ran over to him. He balled his fist and walked toward them.

"Hold on, Nastee," Terrible Trav said, as he grabbed him.

Nastee looked at Venom and asked. "Whoever did this shit to my son is dead. You hear me dead."

"I think I know who might have had orchestrated this," Venom said.

"Who?" Nastee asked.

"Let's step outside what I'm about to tell you is not for everyone's ears."

They stepped outside and Venom told Nastee about Blammer approaching Scar about Faury's death and how they had words and then the shoot-out and the murders of the honor student and Young Josh.

Nastee couldn't believe that Scar was responsible for shooting both of his sons. "I let the first one slide, but not this one" Nastee said, as he picked up the phone and called his mentor. He knew this person knew

Academy Homes better than those who lived in the housing project.

Chapter 39

Mud was the name that inspired hatred, fear and begrudging respect in the city of Detroit. He had bullish shoulders, a bald head, and a sinister smile. There was no man more calculating, cold hearted, and relentless than him in the city of Detroit. His job was to send troops to new grounds to get money, perform murder shows, and set examples. He had a limp from a shoot-out, decades earlier that he would never forget.

Mud was once part of the defunct Y.B.I. (Young Boys Incorporated) drug gang. He was sent to Boston by his boss to attempt to seize the heroin market. His stay in Boston was short, after he received the call that his boss was murdered; he came back to Detroit, took over the top spot and split the faction in two. He took those who were loyal to his team and changed the name of the organization to Cash Flow Inc. Mud was just one of the many monsters walking the streets of Detroit. His propensity for violence was similar to the Best Friends murder for hire crew. His tenacious ability to track down and savagely murder his enemies became legendary. Even the worst of the worst killers applauded his gunplay.

Mud had his phone to his ear listening to Nastee explain the murder of his son Blammer and how he wanted to find Scar and murder him. He asked Nastee a little more about Scar and learned that Scar was the one who had murdered his oldest son as well. He also learned that Uncle Stretch was Scar's father and a grin came over his face. Mud waited for the day to exact revenge on Uncle Stretch and there would be no sweeter way than to murder his son in cold blood.

Mud looked at his brother, Dirt and smiled. He finished the call and stood up. "In a few days we are going to Boston. There's a few things that needs to be handled." Mud said.

Dirt stood up, walked toward the door and held it open for his brother. Mud walked past his brother into the club. He saw that it was emptying out and stopped at a wall size picture of his former boss "Wonder Walt" and said, "This one's for you."

Chapter 40

The past week Bully been watching Rabbit's little sister go and come from school. He felt the only way he can get to Scar was by the betrayal of one of his Wolf-Pack members. He chose Rabbit because he saw how vulnerable he was and how much he cared about his little sister. Bully sat in a blue Honda Accord across the street from the David E. Ellis Elementary School. He watched as Rabbit's sister turned the corner and walked his way. He stepped out and waited for her to pass him.

"Hey, Sabrina, are you Malcolm's little sister?"

"Yes!" said Rabbit's little sister.

"How is your brother doing?" Bully asked.

"He's doing okay. He's in the house sleeping."

"Oh! When you get home can you tell him that his old friend Billy was asking about him."

"Okay." Sabrina said, as she turned and attempted to walk away.

Bully walked behind her, pulled out his stun gun and stunned her. She fell to the ground and he lifted her off the ground and carried her to the trunk of the Honda. He tossed her in, closed the trunk and got in the driver's seat and sped off. He pulled up to the stash house on Townsend Street and saw Tomb outside. Bully nodded to the trunk. Tomb walked over to the trunk and Bully popped it open and Tomb grabbed Rabbit's little sister out and carried her into the house and laid her on the couch. Bully reached in his pocket and called Sincere to inform him that it was done.

* * * * * *

Sincere was sitting on the benches in Franklin Park with White Boy Bink, Trigga and Nice. They were discussing the show that they were throwing.

"I spoke to the owners of the Roxy in Providence and he said that he has an available date for the third of January. That leaves us with a little over a month to get things situated. I will handle the media marketing far as the newspapers, and radio is concerned. The only thing I need y'all to do is to make sure all the clubs, restaurants and beauty salons in Mass and Rhode Island get notice of the event."

"We can do that. What day do the third fall under?" Trigga asked.

"It's on a Saturday."

"Perfect. I will get the flyers and posters printed and then we will work our magic."

"Sounds like a plan." Trigga said, as he thought about the day, he had seen Scar on the Dark Side. He knew if Scar showed up, he can easily be murdered and that's what he intended to do. *"After this event only then can my brother Rest in Peace."* Sincere thought.

Chapter 41

Mud and his little brother Dirt landed in Boston a couple days after speaking to Nastee. They immediately went to meet Nastee at the Copley Hotel. Mud had on a black waist length mink coat, black gator shoes, a pair of slacks and a dress shirt. He sat on a hotel bed listening to Nastee explain all that he had learned from Venom. Mud listened and directed his brother to accompany Nastee on finding members of Scar's family. They walked outside of the hotel and got in Nastee's Escalade.

* * * * * * *

The nail technicians at Tiffany Nail Salon were busy doing manicures and pedicures. In the waiting area customers were breezing through fashion magazines while others were chatting on their cell phones. Baby Fe was getting her nails done by her favorite nail technician Cathy.

Cathy was a short, long haired Vietnamese female with large breasts. She was the owner of the nail salon, Tiffany's. She named the shop after her little sister. She was a business woman who had six nail salons across the city and two in suburban towns. She enjoyed working in her newest shops and had plans to open another a few blocks away.

Nastee, Terrible Trav and Dirt was on a mission to find, shoot, or snatch anyone associated with Scar. Nastee sped up Blue Hill Avenue and passed the welcome to Grove Hall sign. He hit his left blinker and took the turn onto Washington Street. He saw Baby Fe's X-5 BMW parked outside of a nail salon.

"Bingo. There goes that bitch Baby Fe. This will make that little nigga show his face," Nastee said, as he hit the brakes, reached in his waist and pulled out a gun. He stepped out and marched into the nail salon followed by Terrible Trav and Dirt. He stood at the entrance of the shop scanning faces of the customers. He mumbled a few words when he saw who he was looking for getting her nails done at the third booth. Cathy paused as she saw Nastee stomping toward them. Before she could say anything, he was towering over Baby Fe with a gun in his left hand.

Terrible Trav stood at the door and made sure that the front of the shop was in order while Dirt made sure no one dashed out of the back. Baby Fe turned around on the stool and was slapped out of her seat. Nastee stood over her and slapped her hard across the face and then he grabbed her by the throat.

"Tell your punk ass son to come out of hiding. Tell him to face me, man to man," Nastee said, as he squeezed her neck as if he was ready to snap it.

The scared customers watched in horror as Baby Fe's body dangled above the stool. Nastee choke slammed her body hard to the floor. The loud thud was heard next door in the beauty salon. Nastee pointed the gun at Baby Fe with intentions to pull the trigger.

"I'm a gee, this bitch has no role in her son's actions," he thought, "THAT WOULD BRING HIS PUNK ASS OUT OF HIDING" Nastee yelled, as he turned around and faced Cathy, "GIVE ME THE TAPE."

Terrible Trav grabbed Cathy by her collar and walked her to the back. A few minutes later he came back with the disk in his hand. Nastee turned around and stormed out the door slamming it hard. The force of the slam shattered the glass door. Cathy ran to Baby Fe and picked her head up. She saw the bruises and noticed she was unconscious. She started to cry and spoke in Cantonese to her sisters to call 911.

Chapter 42

Tay pulled up in her driveway, parked, stepped out and entered her house. She walked inside the bathroom, brushed her teeth and goggled. She spit the contents in the toilet and looked in the mirror at her pretty face. Next she cut on the shower and stepped in. Fifteen minutes later stepped out and walked inside the living room and plopped down on the sofa.

"I'm tired as hell," Tay said, as she closed her eyes and dozed off.

An hour later Tay was awoken by her ringer. She picked up the phone and listened to her mother inform her about what had happened to her little sister and her condition. She hopped off the couch, got dressed and tossed on a pink and white leather jacket, some timberlands and left. She drove down the highway with tears in her eyes hoping that her little sister would be okay. She made it to Boston Medical Center in record breaking time and pulled next to her mother's Escalade. She stepped out and rushed into the hospital.

Tay stepped inside the emergency room and was greeted by a bevy of Cincinnati Reds Caps. She saw over a dozen people in support for her sister and by passed the crowd and stepped onto the elevator. Tay's mother was in the hallway when Tay stepped off the elevator. She saw her daughter and waved her hand. Tay saw her mother and hurried toward the room to where her sister was at. She reached her mother, gave her a hug and walked inside the room. She caught sight of her sister laid up with a gauze pad wrapped around her head and bruises covering her neck.

"Who did this to you?" Tay asked.

"Nastee," Baby Fe answered.

"I can't believe this nigga would do this sucker shit." Tay said, as she looked at the condition her sister was in, she couldn't help but to think about the conversation that her and Nastee had while he was incarcerated after he found out about the death of his son. Tay replayed the conversation that she had with Nastee on a visit in state prison after their son was killed in her head.

"Do you think it's acceptable that your nephew killed my son?"

"What you mean acceptable? That was an accident. You make it seem like it was done on purpose."

261

"Accident or purpose. The fact is that I lost a son."

"No! We lost a son. I know you are feeling fucked up about this just like I am. How do you think I feel about my nephew being involved?"

"If I was out then this would have had been rectified."

"Rectified. What the fuck are you talking about? You nor anyone else is going to do anything to my nephew. This was an accident and I came here to talk to you about our lost and instead you came out talking this bullshit. Insinuating like it wasn't an accident."

"I'm not insinuating anything. I lost my son and you sit here protecting the little bastard who did it.

"Byron, I'm going through too much to sit here and argue with you. I was called to the grand jury and must testify about what happened. My lies have led to me and my son getting arrested. You can say what you want but I know you aren't going to do nothing to my nephew."

"Tay. You are changing on me and I don't like it."

"This nigga lied to me, he said that he would never hurt my family. Where's Scar at?" Tay asked, as she pulled a chair up to her sister's bed and sat down.

"Ma, just called him and told him what had happened." Baby Fe said.

* * * * * *

Scar was at Kia's apartment when he received a call from his grandmother about what happened to his mother. He was shocked to hear that someone would harm his mother. He gave dap to Rabbit and Pitt and left Kia's apartment. He walked to the Walgreens parking lot.

As he walked to his car, he looked over his shoulder and reached for the door handle of his rental car.

"BOOM." The first shot shattered the window.

Scar ducked and hit the ground as three more shots hit the car. He reached in his waist, pulled out his .40 Sig Sauer Handgun, and got around the car. He noticed there was two shooters.

"BOOM! BOOM! BOOM!" Three more shots flew his way.

The three shots penetrated the hood of Scar's car. From Scar's angle he was able to get a clear look at one of the shooters. He saw Monster coming close with his gun aimed. Scar raised his hand, pulled the trigger, and fired three shots. One caught Monster in the left leg. Monster screamed, fired off two more shots, and retreated. Scar came around the car and caught the other shooter peering in Monster's direction.

"*Mistake, Mistake,*" Scar thought.
Scar aimed, hit his target, and watched as he fell backward. He ran up on him, aimed his pistol at his head, and noticed it was Clapper from Lucerne Street.

"I'm going to fuck the shit out of Disney tonight," Scar said sarcastically before pulling the trigger.

"BOOM! BOOM! BOOM!"

* * * * * *

Rabbit was on his way to the Light Side when he heard a distant sound of gunshots.

"Damn, niggas are getting busy," he said, as he saw Sincere standing outside of a building. He stopped and greeted Sincere. "What's up Sin?"

"What's up with you. How is your family doing?" Sincere asked.

"They good. You know my mom passed away last year." Rabbit said.

"Bless her soul she was a good lady." Sincere said.

"It's just me and my little sister. I'm doing my best to take care of her, it's hard but somebody gotta do it."

"You can do it youngster. How are you supporting yourself?"

"I'm getting a little bread out here to take care of my little sis, but I'm out here just repping the Acadz for life."

"Let's take a walk I need to talk to you" Sincere insisted, as he wrapped his arm around Rabbit's shoulder, "your focus should be getting money to take care of your sis. You are all she got dawg. Don't be a follower and get bagged on some dumb shit and leave her out here in these streets," Sincere said, as he led Rabbit to Marcella Park "I see you little niggas been putting in a lot of work around here, holding the project down and murdering everything moving. I respect that, but it's too much gunplay, little homey."

"That's what we do! Can't stop, won't stop, big homey!" Rabbit responded, as they crossed Washington Street and walked down

Marcella Street. As they neared Marcella Park Rabbit saw Bully and Tomb leaning on Bully's BMW. They walked over toward the BMW.
"What's up my gees, Rabbit said, as he gave them dap.
"What's up Rabbit. What's up with your man Scar?" Bully asked, as he looked Rabbit in the eyes.

Rabbit knew something was up and placed his hand in his pocket. He gripped the .380 in case he had to shoot through his shirt. He had no problems with dusting someone off if his life depended on it, but one thing for sure was that he was not going to give any information about any Wolf Pack Member.
"I don't know." Rabbit answered.
"There's been a lot of disloyalty in the project lately," Tomb cut in.
"So, what are you saying? There's no loyalty in the project?" Rabbit asked.
"Yeah!" Bully said with an attitude.

Sincere sat back smiling at what he created. He knew Bully wanted to kill anyone who had Scar's back. He stepped forward and pulled Rabbit to the side. He reached in his pocket and passed him a fist full of hundred-dollar bills. "That's you, little homey. Over there, under the bleachers is one hundred grams of cocaine for you. It's free of charge."
"I'm not setting up no one from the Wolf Pack for you," Rabbit said.
"The Wolf Pack don't care about you. They scream loyalty but look at your' appearance. They scream unification, but you don't get money like Riot, Scar or Pitt. You can't see you're a tool," Sincere said.

"You kill Scar, we front you the heroin, coke, or whatever else you want. How else you going to pay the ransom for ya little sister?" Tomb said.

"Ransom?" Rabbit asked confused.

"Yeah! Ransom. Earlier when your sister was walking to school a friend of mines scooped her up." Sincere said, as he started to laugh.

"Yeah! Right," Rabbit said.

"BULLY," Sincere shouted.

Bully reached in his pocket and pulled out a cell phone. He dialed a number and put it on speaker. Rabbit heard his little sister's voice calling out his name and lowered his head.

"Damn!" Rabbit scolded himself.

Rabbit scratched his fuzzy single braids came to his conclusion. He agreed to the proposal that Sincere made, walked over and picked up the cocaine, and headed back to the project.

Little Barry from the Wolf Pack was coming out of the project, saw Rabbit, looked and saw Bully's BMW skirting off.

"Where you coming from?" Little Barry asked.

Rabbit jumped back a few feet, looked at one of his fellow Wolf Pack members, and stuttered. "The store."

Little Barry saw no evidence that he had come from the store and decided to inquire further. "Why didn't you go to the store in the project? We have two?" Little Barry asked.

"I needed to clear my head, so I walked to the store on Marcella Street." Rabbit responded.

"You know someone got murked outside of Walgreens." Little Barry said.

"That's what happened. I heard some gunshots earlier."

"Yeah! Someone got smacked. Better him than me," Little Barry said.

Rabbit knew if he didn't do what Sincere asked immediately, that his little sister would be the next body at the city morgue. "I'm about to head to the crib and get some rest," Rabbit said, as he gave Little Barry dap and walked away. *"I'm getting my little sister back by any means even if I have to murk Scar by myself,"* Rabbit said to himself.

Chapter 43

Scar stashed the gun in the woods and went to Kia's house. He pulled Pitt to the side and told him what had happened. Scar waited for twenty minutes and then called a taxi. He stood by the window waiting for his taxi. The taxi pulled up and he gave Pitt dap and walked to the taxi.

"I'm bugging. I smacked a nigga in broad day light. I wonder if anyone saw me. I have to fall back, this is my third murder in months and I'm not going to keep getting away with this shit," Scar said to himself, as he opened the taxi door and slid in the backseat. He directed the driver to Boston Medical Center.

The taxi pulled up to Boston Medical Center. Scar paid the fare, stepped out and walked inside the hospital. He saw a few people from his mother's neighborhood and stopped. He said a few words to them and learned that his mother was attacked at a local nail salon. He thanked them for the information and headed toward her room. He found the room and walked inside and saw his grandmother and his Aunt Tay sitting in chairs beside his mother's bed. The sight of the bandages his mother had wrapped around her head made him angry. Scar gave his aunt and grandmother hugs and kisses. He walked over to his mother's bedside.

"Ma! You alright?" Scar asked, as he bent down and kissed her.

"Yeah! I'm okay. I'm in a little pain, but I will be alright. I'm glad that you made it here. Grab a chair and sit down."

"What happened?" Scar asked, as he grabbed a chair and sat beside his mother.

"Baby, I was getting my nails done and Nastee came into the shop and slapped me out of my seat and then he picked me up by my throat and slammed me hard to the floor," Baby Fe said, as she shed a tear.

Scar stood up, turned around and walked toward the door. He heard his mother shout his name.

"SHYHEIM. WHERE YOU GOING?"

Scar ignored her calls and walked outside of the room. He knew that the war was now on and only the best man would win.

"After I kill Monster, I'm killing Nastee then I'm going to live with

270

my father in Arizona."

Chapter 44

The next morning the nurse entered Baby Fe's room and saw her looking toward the window, staring into space. The nurse looked at her concerned and asked. "Is everything alright Ms. Davis?"

"Yes! I'm fine." Baby Fe answered.
"You are being discharged this morning."
"Yes. That's the understanding I had, from the doctor." Baby Fe retorted.

The nurse turned around and left. Baby Fe has been concerned about her son since she had informed him that Nastee was responsible for her injuries because he had not returned or since been in touch. Baby Fe pulled out her cell phone and called her sister Tay.

"Hello!" Tay answered.

"It's me." Baby Fe said.

"How you feeling this morning?" Tay asked.

"The doctor said, I'm fine. They are discharging me."

Tay heard the urgency and concern in her sister's voice and said. "Okay. I'll be there."

Baby Fe finished the call with her sister and called her son. Scar sat in the living room at Abby's apartment watching the news when his phone rang. He saw his mother's number. He answered and spoke to her briefly. An hour later he got up from the couch, gave Abby a kiss and walked to the door. He opened it and left the apartment. He took a taxi to Norwood and went inside the house to wait for his mother. When he walked in, he was surprised to see his mother sitting on the couch.

"Hey baby" Baby Fe greeted.

"Hey ma" Scar said, as he hugged his mother. A tear fell down his face. He couldn't believe that his actions from long ago led to a chain of events that caused his mother to be hospitalized. He loved his mother and believed she and his pops were the only ones who truly cared about him. He wiped the tears and released his grip.

Now ma! Can you explain everything that happened and explain to me everything you know about Nastee?"

"Baby, I still can't believe that Nastee had done that to me. What happened was I was at Tiffany's getting my nails done and when I looked Nastee was standing behind me with a gun in his hand."

"He had a gun?" Scar asked.

"Yes! He slapped me out of the chair onto the ground, then he slapped me hard across my face and then he picked me up by my throat and started yelling to tell you to come out of hiding and to face him man to man and then he slammed me hard to the ground and then I went unconscious."

"*I'm killing this nigga and all his crew*" Scar thought, "what type of gangster go at a niggas mother." Scar said.

"Nastee, is a man who played by no rules. I know because my sister was with him for ten years. He liked going to war and takes it seriously. He likes killing and he's real strategic." Baby Fe said.

Scar felt his phone vibrate, excused himself and looked at the screen saver. He saw that it was Rabbit and answered. Scar was informed that Rabbit knew Monster's whereabouts and wanted to talk to him. He agreed to meet him on the Dark Side. He walked back over to his mother.

"Ma, how did you get home?"

"Your aunt dropped me off, she stepped out for a minute and will be back any minute." Baby Fe said, as she heard her door open.

Tay walked in and saw her nephew Scar. "Hey Shyheim, I'm glad that you are here to support your moms. She really needs you and I know you are mad about what had happened, but you have to be careful out here too cause Nastee is a mad man and when he gets angry then he is practically unstoppable and could get real nasty and relentless. I know what you're thinking, just let the lord handle this. Shyheim, Nastee is fearless and treasures gunplay.

"How do you feel about what he had done to my mom?" Scar asked.

"I don't approve of him putting his hands on my little sister. I left him alone after he threatened me in prison."

"Threatened you how?"

"It's a long story. I will tell you one day."

"Okay."

"Now listen I know you think you know what you're doing out here in these streets and all but promise me you will call your father before you do anything foolish." Baby Fe said.

"Ma! I don't want to involve my dad in this." Scar said.

"Boy trust me your father and Broad Day Jay know the things you need to hear and know about how serious Nastee's gangster really is." Baby Fe informed.

Scar did as he told his mother he would do and called his father. He agreed to spend from Thanksgiving until New Years in Arizona with him. After he got off the phone with his father, he received a call from Rabbit about Monster's whereabouts. He smiled knowing that today was the day that he would finally murder one of his worst enemies.

"He got away the other day, but this time I'm killing him," Scar said, as he tossed on a black T-shirt, strapped on his Kevlar Vest, and placed a holster on his shoulder. He grabbed his Jericho and placed it in the holster. He picked up his black Army fatigue jacket, black skull cap and put them on. He walked into the living room, and kissed his mother and aunt.

"Ma, I'm about to go out, can I use your car for a few hours?"
"Yes baby, be careful you hear me. The keys are on my dresser in the room. Scar drove to the Dark Side and during the whole ride he thought about the recent rash of violence that he had created and shook his head. "I'm out here murking niggas left and right. I need to slow down before I get bagged for one of these shits."

Scar made it to Boston and drove to Egleston Square and pulled on Atherton Street and saw Rabbit sitting on some stairs outside of a house. It's been 36 hours since Rabbit's little sister was kidnapped, and he was beginning to stress. He saw Scar pull up and walked over to the car and slid in the passenger seat. They drove to Orchard Park Housing Project.

Scar noticed how nervous Rabbit was and didn't understand why he was acting so jittery. Scar was starting to feel a bad vibe when he pulled up inside an alley across the street from Orchard Park Project.

"Come on," Scar said, as he opened the door and stepped out.
"They be right over here," Rabbit said, as he walked toward the mouth of the alley.

Scar looked and saw Monster on a set of crutches along with a few members of his project. He counted them and stopped at thirteen. *"This is going to be sweet, I'm sure to strike gold tonight."*

"Do you have your vest on?" Rabbit asked.

"Nah!" Scar answered.

Scar found the question unusual and decided to keep an eye on Rabbit, "I'm going to take the lead," Scar said, as he pulled out his gun. He raised his gun and pulled the trigger. He turned around and ran back inside the alley and couldn't believe his eyes. "What the fuck," he said, as he saw Rabbit pointing a gun at his chest.

"BOOM! BOOM!"

The two slugs propelled Scar backward and over a crate. The air was gone from his lungs before he hit the ground. Scar's head hit the pavement and his eyes rolled back in his head as his body went limp.

Rabbit couldn't believe that he had shot and killed Scar. He stepped forward, lowered the gun and shot Scar two more times in the chest. He turned around and walked toward a Honda Civic that he had parked there earlier. Unknown to him, earlier in the day a few kids were playing and broke the tail light. He opened the door, climbed in, reached his hand under the passenger seat, and grabbed a plastic bag. He placed the gun and gloves in the bag and tossed it on the passenger seat. He dialed Bully's number and informed him that he had killed Scar in an alley near Orchard Park. He pulled off, drove down the street and was caught in a traffic jam.

A few cars behind him was the detective Red Beard in a black Bronco. Rabbit looked in his rear view and switched lanes. Red Beard spotted the traffic violation as Rabbit switched lanes and flicked on his lights. Rabbit panicked and drove off at top speed. The only thing on his mind was getting rid of the murder weapon. He took a left and drove into St. Joseph Housing Development and pulled the emergency brake. The car skidded and came to a stop. He grabbed the bag and hopped out. He ran and tried to toss the bag over a fence. The toss was too short as it hit the fence and fell on the ground. He jumped and tried to scale the 12-foot fence but was grabbed by Red Beard and pulled down. He was cuffed and walked to the Bronco. Red Beard's partner ran, grabbed the bag, and opened it. He looked in, pulled out the gun and shouted.

"WE GOT A GUN."

* * * * * *

Scar's eye-lids fluttered and then snapped open. He attempted to focus, but his vision was blurred. His senses slowly came back one at a time. He tried to move but the pain was excruciating in his head and chest. Scar laid on his back and stared up at the dimly lit sky. His first reaction was to try to sit up. The pain in his chest forced him to lay back down. He rolled over on his left side and grabbed a railing for leverage. He got up one knee at a time.

"That motherfucker," Scar mumbled.

Scar touched the back of his head then ran his fingers outside and down the front of the hoodie and felt four slugs that had been caught by his vest. He cursed himself for letting Rabbit destroy his vest. He vowed to stab Rabbit to death, pour gasoline in his eyes, and light him on fire.

"Son of a bitch," he said, as he examined his vest.

Scar saw his gun on the ground, picked it up, staggered to the car and climbed in. He sat for a few seconds, heard some sirens, and then drove off. He saw some cruisers fly past him. He took a few turns, saw a half dozen police cruisers down St. Joseph and went the opposite direction. He took a right on Washington Street and drove past Dudley Square.

"I can't believe this nigga tried to kill me. I'm going to kill his bitch ass."

Scar drove down Harrison Avenue and turned into Cathedral Project and parked outside of Abby's building. He stepped out and walked into the building. He opened the door and saw Abby counting money that Jose had given her for the heroin he sold.

"It's all here" Abby said, as she looked up at Scar. "What's wrong? What happened?" She asked getting up.

"Punk ass Rabbit tried to murk me. I think them older niggas put him up to it," Scar said, taking off his hoodie and then his vest.

Abby looked at the holes in his vest, "you trust all these niggas when I should be the only one you trust." She said in a stern manner.

"Don't worry next time I see him he's a dead man," Scar said, as he sat on the edge of the couch with his chest aching. "I'm about to clean myself up and get some rest. When these bruises go down, I'm killing one of them faggots." Scar seethed as he got up from the couch and walked inside the bathroom.

Chapter 45

Soon as Sincere received the news that Rabbit had gotten arrested, he immediately alerted Bully to release Rabbit's sister. He didn't want Rabbit to snitch and finger him for the abduction of the little girl. Sincere couldn't believe that Rabbit had got caught that fast.

It's been three weeks since Rabbit's arrest and now that the coast was clear and no arrest has been made in the disappearance of Rabbit's little sister Sincere came out of hiding and returned back to his project. He pulled up and parked on Dimock Street. He stepped out and walked to the corner of Dimock Street and Columbus Avenue.

"Damn, this will be my first Thanksgiving and Christmas out in three years. I need to gather all my kids up and spend the holiday with my mom's." Sincere said, as he pulled out his cell phone and ordered some clam strips from Star Fish Market.

Sincere decided to walk to the fish market as rain started to lightly drizzle. He walked down Columbus Avenue and crossed the intersection and walked toward the fish market.

"Look at bitch ass Sincere sleeping." Scar said, as he saw Sincere walk inside the fish market. "Baby find a parking spot. I need to holler at this nigga."

Abby did what Scar asked and drove down the street and found a parking spot.

Sincere walked in, grabbed his order and stepped out. He walked back to the project and stopped. He was so into eating his clam strips that he never noticed a car following him. He opened the bag and pulled out a few clam strips. As he tossed them in his mouth, a voice greeted him.

"Peace God," Scar said, as he reached his arm out of the window and pumped six shots into Sincere upper body. He fell to the ground and started twitching. Scar pulled his arm inside the car and leaned back. Abby made a wild U-turn on Columbus Avenue and steered the car toward Bragdon Street. She parked and they hopped out of the stolen car and got into Abby's car that was parked on Ernst Street and sped off. Light drizzle continued to hit the ground as a crowd formed around Sincere's body as he stared into the sky with lifeless eyes.

* * * * * * *

Mr. Homicide was in his office when he got the call about Sincere's murder. He raced out of his office and hopped in his car. He drove to the murder scene and parked. He saw the coroner truck parked not too far from the white sheet that covered the body. He stepped out, walked over to where the body laid under a white sheet. He bent down, lifted the sheet and saw Sincere's lifeless body. He recognized Sincere's face and knew that there would be retaliation. He walked over to a few other homicide detectives.

"This has the smell of a gang war. I want this whole area shut down. There have been too many murders in this vicinity, and I don't like it. Any car coming in and out of either side of the housing project I want pulled over, searched and if anybody has even a seed of marijuana, I want them arrested. Also, I will speak to the mayor about placing a curfew in this neighborhood. The people who have been murdered around here are high ranking members who were high on the Impact Player list."

The detectives shook their heads as they listened to Mr. Homicide. He walked over to a few witnesses who saw the shooting and asked a female with long black hair that was pulled back in a pony-tail a few questions. He listened as she described the car the shooter was in and how it escaped down Bragdon Street. Mr. Homicide told a few of his detectives to drive around the Bragdon Street area and search for the car. He thanked the witnesses and walked to his car. He saw his partner in the passenger seat writing in his notepad. He opened the door and sat in the driver's seat. He ran his hand over his face.

"Damn, there are too many unsolved murders in this area. These guys are feeling invisible. Five murders and ten shootings in less than six months don't look good on our part." Mr. Homicide said to his partner. "It seems like this neighborhood has a code of silence. It doesn't look good at all. The captain is breathing down our backs, the commissioner is breathing down his back and now the Feds want to investigate the activity in this neighborhood. Did the shot spotters and surveillance cameras get installed?"

"Not yet! But they will." His partner said.

"It might take months, even years, but when I'm finished with these guys, they will be spread across the country in federal prisons."

Chapter 46

Bully received a call that Sincere had been shot on Columbus Avenue. Bully chirped Tomb and told him what happened and to meet him in the Walgreens parking lot. Bully got in his Cadillac Escalade and pulled off. Ten minutes later he pulled up into the parking lot and seen Tomb and a few others standing in the lot in tears. He stepped out and walked toward them. He saw the tears in Tomb's eyes and pulled him to the side. He listened as Tomb told him about the account of what happened from one of the witnesses and how the shooter drove down Bragdon Street. Bully listened as tears welled up in his eyes. He looked and saw a coroner truck parked where Sincere's body laid under a white sheet.

"So, he was dead on arrival?" Bully asked.

Without saying a word Tomb shook his head. A tear came down Bully's face. He looked at Tomb and said. "I got a feeling that bitch ass nigga Scar had something to do with this. I want a ten thousand price tag on his head."

"There's no need for a price tag. I'm going to kill that nigga myself. I will honor your word and spread the word." Tomb said.

"Next time we see that nigga it's on. It's shoot on sight. I know this is his work," Bully said, as he gave Tomb a pound and walked away. "I know what I have to do." Bully said, as he looked up to the sky and said, "rest in peace Sincere."

* * * * * *

Abby drove to her apartment and saw Jose outside hustling in a red snorkel coat. She parked and they stepped out. They walked over to Jose and gave him dap.

"What's up? How is everything looking?" Scar asked.

"It's moving. They love this Skull Crush. I'm almost done. I have a few bundles left then I will be coming to see you."

"That's good to hear. I'm going to be gone for a while so deal with Abby, she will make sure you are alright."

"Okay." Jose said, as he greeted Abby, "What's up sis?"

"I'm glad to hear that it's a great day" Abby smiled, as she hugged Jose.

"Alright. I'll see you in a few." Jose informed.

"Okay. You know where I'm at." Abby said, as she walked away.

Jose watched Abby and Scar walk inside her building. He turned and walked to a project bench and sat down. Scar and Abby walked up the stairs and into the apartment. Scar took off his coat and hoodie and sat on the couch and said. "I'm going to dip and visit my father. I don't know who seen what and really don't give a fuck. I must call Logan Airport and see when the next plane to Phoenix leaves. While I'm gone, I need you to continue to bless Jose with the bundles he needs and all you have to do is collect the money and bless him with more dope" Scar said, as he grabbed some underclothes, his phone charger and stuffed it inside a small black bag.

"I can handle that. When are you leaving?"

"I'm trying to leave within the next few hours. "

"How long are you going to be gone?" Abby asked.

"I don't know a few weeks; a few months it all depends on how things go with my father."

"So, you going to spend the holidays there?" Abby asked.

"Yeah and probably a little bit longer."

"So, what about me. I'm not going to bring in the New Year with you?"

"I want to spend the New Year with you, but you know what I'm about to do. This will be only the second time that I spent with my dad since I have been home. This meeting I'm going to have with him is serious. I don't want to tell him everything, but I do value his wisdom" Scar said, as he pulled out his phone and dialed the airport's toll-free number. He listened as the automated voice told him what he wanted to hear. He ended the call and looked at Abby, "the plane leaves in four hours. Come here and give me some of that good pussy" Scar said, as he stood up and grabbed Abby's hand and led her to the bedroom.

They walked into the bedroom and Scar untied his Timberland boots and kicked them off. He pulled down his pants, tossed them on the floor and then took off his boxers. He watched Abby strip out of her clothes and climb onto the bed. He walked toward the bed and smiled at how pretty Abby's pussy was. *"Damn, everything about this bitch is beautiful."* He thought, as he climbed onto the bed and spread her legs wide and slid in her pussy slowly. Abby wrapped her arms around his neck and met his strokes with her own.

"Damn, this pussy is good." Scar said, as he pumped harder and faster. "Ouch Papi! Kill this choca! Kill this choca!" Abby screamed.

Scar felt his nut rising and pumped a few more times and then exploded inside Abby's warm pussy. He pulled out and stuffed his dick in her mouth and closed his eyes as she gave him one of the best blow jobs he ever had. He cummed in her mouth and pulled out and sat on the edge of the bed.

"You need me to take you to the airport? Abby asked.
"Nah baby! I'm going to take a taxi and I will call you once I'm in the terminal."

Scar got dressed and called a taxi and walked to the living room and stood by the window. Abby came out of the bedroom in a long t-shirt and hugged Scar by the waist.

"I love you papi" Abby said, as she kissed the back of Scar's neck.

"I love you Mami." Scar said.

"I will hold everything down until you come back."

"I know. When I come back, we are going to do things differently," Scar said, as he saw a yellow taxi pulling up. *"Damn, that was fast."* Scar thought, "That's my ride," he said, as he turned around and kissed Abby on the lips. They swapped tongues for ten seconds. "I will call you when I get there."

"Enjoy your trip and be safe." Abby said.

"I will." Scar said, as he grabbed a small bag and left. *"Damn, this is one thorough bitch,"* Scar thought, as he walked down the stairs and out of the building. He walked to the taxi and looked up and saw Abby staring out of the window. He couldn't help but to love her for she was all he looked for in a female. He blew her an air kiss. "I love that girl," Scar said, as he got inside the taxi.

The whole ride to the airport Scar thought about the drama he had in the city and how this trip would give him time to clear his mind and figure out how to move better and swifter.

Chapter 47

Scar slept the whole plane ride to Phoenix Sky Harbor International Airport. He woke up as the plane was landing. He couldn't wait to see his dad to tell him the chain of events that led him to murder time after time.

"My old man isn't going to believe this shit I'm going through." Scar thought, as he stood up and stretched. He followed the other passengers out of the plane and onto the tarmac. He walked inside the airport and then passed the baggage claim out the door. He saw his father in a cranberry and black silk shirt and some matching trousers. As he neared, he noticed that his father had on all Gucci from the shirt, trousers and shoes.

"What's up dad?" Scar said, as he gave his father a long hug.

"What's up son, we have a lot of talking to do, but first let me get you out of them clothes and into something new.

"Okay." Scar said, as he followed his father to a black on black BMW 8-Series. "I see you like these coupes huh?"

"Like is an understatement. I love pushing the speed limit through these deserts." Uncle Stretch said, as he laughed.

Scar entered the passenger seat and waited for his father to join him. Uncle Stretch slid in the driver's seat and looked at his son.

"Make sure you put on that seat belt."

Scar put on the seat belt and knew he had to be upfront and honest with his father about everything that he is going through in the streets.

"Your mother told me some real troubling things that are going on in your life, but I know she doesn't know everything, but I want to hear it from you."

"Yeah! You know ma, she always assumes the worst when it comes to me."

"That's why I want you out here, so I can spend some time with you and so I can talk to you and find out what's going on with you because I don't want to go to a funeral or visit you in real jail."

"Man, where do I start?" Scar said, as he pondered about what he wanted to tell his father first.

"The beginning. You know I love you and would hate to hear anything happen to you. So, tell me what's going on back home and what are

295

these problems, I'm hearing about."

Scar looked his father in the eyes and wondered if he should tell him about the many people he had killed. *"This is my dad. If anyone has my back, it's this man."* Scar thought, "Dad, most of the problems I had started the first day I came back to the project. I already told you about me and Free, but what I didn't tell you was that on the night of Academy day I was cutting through the Four Squares and saw him, and Bully posted out there. As I walked, he started shooting at me, I ducked, whipped out my piece and blammed back and hit him in the arm. They ran and got away and I dipped back to the Dark Side and laid low."

"Why didn't you tell me about all this when it happened?"

"Dad, I didn't want to pull you into this. I know you are out here getting money and staying out of the way. If I felt I couldn't handle it then I would've called you, but that's not all."

"It's not." Uncle Stretch said, as he raised his eyebrow.

"No. While me and Free was going through our problems I ran into the kid Blammer from the Point at Che Vous and I did what you requested and told him what happened the day his brother was killed. After the talk I thought we squashed it, but the next day I was telling my man Murder about running into Blammer and then Blammer rode past and started shooting at us and I returned fire that ended up getting in a shoot-out with him."

"Damn, you were going through a lot of bullshit since the last time you were here."

"So, after I had shot Free the kid Blammer came around the A and shot an innocent nigga, who is actually an honor student. That poor kid got murdered for wearing an Atlanta Braves Hat that actually stood for his name. That murder alone brought so much attention to the hood. So, after that murder I stayed away from the project and focused on getting money down St. Joseph."

"What you mean getting money? Getting money how?"

"I sell heroin in the Joe's."

"Okay, keep talking."

"After the shoot-out with Free with Blammer I started taking them serious and then a couple months later the older heads tried to ambush me."

"Ambush you. What are you talking about?"

"Yeah! I started back hanging in the project and I guess them niggas was watching me and knew my early morning route to the Joe's. Those niggas had some pretty bitch on their team and sent her to pop me, but as I walked down Thornton Street, I knew something was funny and saw the setup, whipped out and popped the bitch. As I shot the bitch another nigga came from around the corner shooting at me and we got busy in the middle of the street. I backed him up and ran into a yard to switch clips, but as I was putting in another clip a car pulled up and someone shot me in my back. The only thing that saved me was my bullet-proof vest."

"So, you are telling me that you got shot and this is my first-time hearing about all this. Listen, Shyheim I'm your father, not your friend don't you ever hold these types of secrets from me. Why wouldn't you call me. I know because you're a man. You are more like me than I could have imagined. Do you know who I am in these streets? I am a man among men. Niggas know my name; respect my name and I be damned if someone tries to kill my son while I'm out here. Now, let me tell you about this punk ass niggas Free. Back in the days when you were little, matter fact, let's go back further when we was young the older heads took to me and Jay because of our willingness to rep the project beyond the area we controlled in Roxbury. They saw in us the future and gave us everything and Free and others didn't like it but was too scared to say anything to us so instead they spoke behind our backs. I started getting money early so I had the things that they didn't have and this infuriated Free and then one day he tried to talk to your mother when she told him that she was with me he palmed her ass out of spite and she in return spit in his face and then he slapped her. When your moms told me, what happened I came to the project and whipped his ass in front of everyone and warned him if he violated me again it will be taken to another level. A few years after that he started robbing my workers and that's when I shot him three times and ran him out of the project. So, that's why he hates me."

"After the shooting I spent time regrouping at one of my girls crib and then I met this female from Lynn and she asked me did I know Bully and Free. I lied and told her no. The information she gave me was useful, as I was able to plot and plan to get Free and I did one night as he pulled up to the female's house to pick up her sister and that's when I murked his ass."

"Son, that is good that you told me all of this, but don't ever tell anyone else you had killed that man or any other person. Outside of me who you told this to?"

"No one. I did it by myself and kept it to myself until now."

3 Pounds of Pressure 2: When Pressure is Applied

"Outside of me don't mention this to anyone. You can trust me I'm your dad."

"I know that's why I told you."

"Is that everything?"

"Nah! It's kind of heavy. I knew with me killing Free would create further problems with them older heads, so I kept a watch on them and when Sincere came home I believe he made one of my own dawgs shoot me."

"Shoot you. I thought you said that an older head shot you."

"That was the first time. The second time was in an alley near Orchard Park Project. I was going on a M.I. with one of my niggas and as I got busy and turned to run my own man shot me four times in the chest, but once again the vest saved my life."

"Shit, all this is going on without my knowledge, why you didn't think to call me? So, you are telling me all this happened since you been home?"

"Yeah!"

"When your moms told me, something was going on I had no idea it was that heavy. I would have made that trip to come get you. Who is your boy who had shot you and where is he from?"

"His name is Rabbit and he's from the Light Side. The nigga got locked up a few minutes after he shot me. If I'm not going to kill anybody, I'm going to get him, and I can say on Dawgs to that."

"Don't say on Dawgs, because then you would have to do it."

"That's how sure I am that I'm going to kill him. I don't care how long it takes, he's a dead man. Why you think I killed Sincere."

"When Sincere get killed?"

"This morning. I murked his bitch ass before I stepped on the plane."
*"Damn, my little nigga is a murderer. I guess it runs in the family.
I have to keep my little nigga safe before something happens to him."*
Uncle Stretch thought, as he pulled into a circular driveway and
parked outside of a house. He looked at his son and asked. "What is a
real devil?"

Scar thought long and hard and remembered the lessons that his father
had sent to him while he was incarcerated and stated. "A real devil is
any man made weak and wicked or any live grafted germ from the
original is the devil."

"Since you know what a devil is then why do you continuously act
like one when you know how and what made the devil. It perplexes
me that my son is living the life of a devil by committing devilish acts
while his father is living such a glorious and god like life." Uncle
Stretch said as he sat in the driveway staring at his son.

Scar saw the size of the house and how luxurious it looked and turned
to his dad and asked: "You right. I have to do a better job at making a
difference in my life and others around me. It's not about living
devilishly it's about upliftment and making a difference out here in the
world. Dad, this is your house too?" Scar asked changing the subject.

"Nah! Somebody special lives here." Uncle Stretch said, as he opened
the door, stepped out and walked to the front door.

He used his key to open the door and stepped inside. Scar followed his father inside the house and saw standing in the lobby one of the prettiest females his eyes ever seen.

"Damn, this bitch is bad," Scar thought.

Uncle Stretch walked up to the female and hugged and kissed her.
"Selma, this is my son Shyheim."
"Hi! Shyheim, it's finally nice to meet you I heard a lot about you." Selma said, as she hugged Scar.
"Hi! Selma. It's nice to meet you." Scar said, as he stared at her.
"Are you hungry? I'm about to make dinner. Is there anything you prefer?
"I eat anything except pork." Scar said.
"Oh! No. Your father doesn't like me cooking pork." Selma said with a slight giggle.
"Do you know how to make quesadillas?"
"Of course, I do. I'm Mexican. What do you want on it?"
"Chicken and cheese."
"Okay. What about you baby, are you hungry?" Selma said, as she looked at Uncle Stretch.
"Yeah! You can make me one with veggies and cheese."
"Okay. Let me get in this kitchen and start dinner." Selma said, as she turned and walked into the kitchen.

Scar watched her walk away and admired how shapely her butt was.

"Come on son, let's step inside the living room and watch some T.V.,"

Uncle Stretch said, as he led the way toward the living room.

Scar walked inside the living room and was amazed how spacious the room was. He followed his father to a leather sectional couch and sat down.

"You watch college football?" Uncle Stretch asked, as he grabbed the remote and flicked on the television.

"Yeah!" Scar answered. "Dad, can I ask you a question?"

"Go ahead what's on your mind?"

"What is Selma to you? I saw how you hugged and kissed her."

"That's my girl. We have been together for a few years now."

"Do ma know about her?"

"Yeah! I told her about Selma when I planned to move here for good."

"What she say? Was she mad?"

"Well, she was pissed at first, but when I told her all the things Selma did for me, she understood and supported my every move since."

"Oh! Okay."

"Son, Selma presented me with an opportunity of a lifetime. When I first came out here, she introduced me to her uncle, who at the time was one of the biggest drug dealers on the West Coast. Through her uncle I made millions of dollars off selling weed and was able to leave the coke game alone. The money I was making was too good to be true and I knew I had to start investing so me and Selma started our own real estate investment company and started buying property in Nevada and Arizona. I repaid her by paying her college tuition and helping her get her career going."

"What's her career?"

"She's a lawyer."

"Damn, that pretty thang is a lawyer?" Scar asked.

"Yeah! She chose to be an immigration lawyer because she wanted to help her people out. She's a special person in my life without her I won't be where I'm at today. Son, once an opportunity presents itself to you never be scared to jump at it because you never know where it might take you."

"I'm never scared of no opportunities"

"I hope not because they are coming.and when they do seize them and make the best out of each one. When I made the move out here that was the best decision I have ever made in my life."

"Why you say that dad?"

"Look at me. Look at all that I was able to obtain over the years. When I was back home, we were living in the projects. Now I'm living in million-dollar homes. I met some people who changed my life."

"Like who?"

"I met million-dollar investors, businessmen, politicians, athletes, and a host of other people who changed my views of how the rich supposed to live."

"Damn, so this move really made you see life for what it is. It made you change from your old ways."

"Change is not the choice word to describe what happened to me. The proper word is reshaped. I thought I was making money back home, but as I know now, I was making pennies compared to what I made since I came here. When I started seeing them M's I never looked back. I have a newfound respect for the almighty dollar," Uncle

Stretch said, as he laughed, "Now don't get it twisted I was making paper in Boston, but I was stuck in the six-figure bracket. After years of hustling I was able to retire and focus on flipping houses. Do you know how it feels to shake hands with politicians?"

"No."

"You will soon, as you come out here for good. You my son all that I have is yours remember that."

Scar thought about what his father was saying and every time he looked over his shoulder in Boston someone was pointing a gun at him. *"It would feel good not to have that worry no more."* Scar thought. "Dad, I have no problem with moving out here, but I want to clear up this shit with D.Y.S. first. You know they aren't trying to let me relocate."

"I will make a few calls and see what I can do."

"Alright. To be honest, I can't leave my girl Abby back home. I know the saying is true' can't bring sand to the beach, but she's not considered sand she is a diamond in the rough."

"Who said you couldn't bring her with you. I got enough room for both of y 'all."

"That's what I wanted to hear?" Scar said with a smile.

Selma walked inside the living room with two plates of Quesadillas and placed one next to Scar and the other besides Uncle Stretch.

"Is there anything y 'all would like to drink?" Selma asked.

"Yes! Make us some of that fantastic lemonade you make." Uncle Stretch said.

"Okay. I will be right back." Selma said.

As she walked away Scar peeked at her round booty. "Dad you get points for that one."
"To be the best you have the best." Uncle Stretch said with a short laugh.
"I hear that." Scar said, as he thought about Abby.

A few minutes later Selma came back with a tray that had three cups of lemonade and a pita style sandwich. She passed Scar a glass of lemonade and placed her tray next to Uncle Stretch and sat down.

"Shyheim, I heard a lot about you over the years. You are all that your father talks about. I'm glad that you finally decided to make it out here to visit."
"I know. I should be coming out here more often, but a lot of things have been going on back home, but I'm here now."
"So, tell me about you. Did you finish high school?"
"Yes. When I was in the Department of Youth Services, I was able to finish High School."
"What about college? Do you plan to further your education?"
"I'm thinking about going to school for business management."
"That's a good major. What you plan on opening up a business someday?" Selma asked.
"Yeah! I was looking around and realized there weren't too many beauty supply stores and I was thinking about filling that void."
"That's good that you are thinking about becoming an entrepreneur at

your age because most kids your age are focused on being employees instead of the employer. What about real estate? Have you given that any thought?" Selma asked.

"Not really. My dad was telling me how good he is doing in the real estate market and I'm willing to learn the real estate game."

"Well he's the one to see in that game, "Selma said, as she cut her eye at Uncle Stretch and smiled.

"I know. When I get my things in order, I will sit down with him and pick his brain. I see you have an Arizona State shirt on what you a Sun Devils fan?"

"Yes. I love my Sun Devils. That was my team growing up and still is to this day. What's your team?"

"I don't have one, but if I did, I would have to go with the home team Boston College. I like individual players."

"That's no fun cheering for one player. You have to cheer for a team to get the real excitement of the game." Selma said.

"Says who?" Scar asked looking at Selma.

"Me. Esquire Selma Gonzalez." Selma laughed.

Uncle Stretch sat back eating his quesadilla listening to their conversation. He loved how naturally they connected.

"Now, you know about me it's my turn. How long you been a lawyer?" Scar asked.

"I'm on my third year as an immigration lawyer." Selma responded.

"Did you get your law degree at Arizona State?"

"No! I went to UNLV in Nevada."

"I can just imagine all the work and studying you had to do to become a lawyer. That's too much school for me."

"Not if you are trying to make a change for your people." Selma smiled.

"Now, that's different. If it was for a purpose, then I can go to school forever."

"TOUCH DOWN," Selma shouted as she saw her team's quarterback threw a long touchdown pass.

"Make yourself comfortable son, we are going to be spending the next few days between here and my house before we head to Vegas to see Broad Day Jay."

"Alright." Scar said, as he picked up his quesadilla and bit into it.

Chapter 48

Scar woke up the next morning and thought about Abby. *"Damn, I didn't get a chance to call my baby yesterday,"* Scar thought, as he stepped off the bed. He grabbed his toiletry bag and walked to the bathroom that was inside of the bedroom he was sleeping in. He brushed his teeth, washed his face and then took a shower. He finished cleaning himself and walked out of the bathroom and looked at the clock that sat on the nightstand. "9:42am," Scar said, as he picked up his phone and dialed Abby's number.

"Hello." Abby answered the phone on the third ring.

"Hey baby, how are you this morning?"

"Good. I was waiting for your call yesterday. How was your flight?"

"Long, but I needed that long plane ride to clear my head. I meant to call you yesterday, but when I got here, I was talking to my dad and his girlfriend and after I ate, I fell asleep. What's up with Jose?"

"He's out here shaking. They are loving him these days." Abby laughed.

"That's good to hear. I don't know when I'm coming back, but when I do, I'm going to look to invest in some sort of business. My dad is the man out here, you should see the way he is living. What's up with the situation with ole boy."

Abby knew Scar was inquiring about what happened to Sincere.

"I spoke to Kia and she told me that the word on the street was that the Bragdon niggas had something to do with it since they found the car where them guys hang at."

"Oh, alright." Scar said, as he smiled, "keep your ears and eyes open.

"Alright. How is the weather there?" Abby asked.

"It's nice in the low eighties." Scar answered.

"Damn, I'm jealous," Abby laughed, "it's chilly as hell out here."

"That sucks. What are you doing today?"

"Nothing, just waiting on Jose to bring some money and watch a few television shows."

"Baby let me get dressed and eat breakfast with my pops," Scar said, "I'll call you a little later. I love you."

"I love you more," Abby said, as she hung up.

"Damn, I love that girl," Scar thought, as he placed the phone on the nightstand. He got dressed and then walked toward the kitchen and saw his father sitting in the sun room reading a Wall Street Journal.

"Good morning dad," Scar said, as he walked toward his father.

"Good morning son," Uncle Stretch said, as he folded the paper, stood up and gave his son a hug. "I know you are hungry so there's some fresh fruit, in the kitchen for you. For lunch we are going to go out to a Vegan restaurant. I want to show you how to start eating healthy."

Scar grabbed some grapes, sliced peaches and a piece of mango and joined his father in the sun room. He admired the way his father moved, lived and conducted business.

"So tell me about this Abby of yours?"

"She is a Boricua wait till you meet her you will love her."

"Is she from Academy?"

"Nah! She is from Philly but has been living in Cathedral for a few years now. She's a complete package dad. She's pretty, smart and ride or die."

"It sounds like you have a winner on your arms. How did y'all meet?"

"Through Pitt's girl Kia from the A. The first day we met I took her on a MI so that she can prove herself."

"Do you think that was a good idea?" Uncle Stretch asked shaking his head.

"Now that I think about it, no. It was dumb to do that, but what's done is done. She proved herself that day and many times after. I can't help but to love her. I wanted to bring her down here with me, but I knew this was our time."

"She's always welcome to my home. If she's who you say she is then she is welcome in my home. What made her leave Philly?"

"She has family in the South End and decided to relocate to be close to them."

"Alright. When you finish eating, I want to show you a few pieces of real estate I own and teach you a few things so that you can have that general knowledge of the real estate market.

Chapter 49

The next few weeks Uncle Stretch showed Scar all the real estate he owns in Arizona and taught him the basics of the real estate game. Scar soaked up all the information that his father was teaching him and decided once he got his affairs in order that he would invest the money he made into real estate.

"You ready, to go and spend time in Nevada with your godfather?"
"Yeah!" Scar said, as he got up from the sofa and followed his father out of the house.

Scar walked to the passenger door of his father's Seven Series BMW and opened the door and slid in. "How long is the ride dad?"
"Six hours."

"Damn, that's a troop." Scar said, as he reclined the seat back.
"What you want to listen to?" Uncle Stretch asked.
"Chief Keef, Lil Bibby, Lil Durk or anyone from Chicago."
Scar said.

Uncle Stretch pulled up the Pandora app and said Lil Durk's name.
The six hours flew as Scar sat in the passenger seat and listened to all
the rappers from Chicago.

"We here." Uncle Stretch said, as he drove down Las Vegas
Boulevard. He pulled up to the Venetian Hotel and parked out front.
Scar unbuckled his seat belt and stepped out. He watched his father
hand the car keys to the valet and they walked inside the casino. They
walked through the casino toward the bar. Scar looked at all the pretty
waitresses walking around. Scar saw Broad Day Jay sitting at the bar
sipping on a glass of champagne.

Broad Day Jay saw Uncle Stretch and Scar coming his way and
downed the rest of the champagne. He stood up and hugged each one
of them and looked Scar in the eyes and asked.

"Little nigga, you ready to get something to eat."
"Yup." Scar answered.

Broad Day Jay led the way toward Otto Enoteca Pizzeria restaurant.
They walked inside and stopped at the counter. Scar saw a few large
slices of pizza on display behind the counter. He saw that one of the

slices of pizza had pineapples on it and wondered how that tasted.

"You still like Buffalo Chicken pizza," Uncle Stretch asked, as he remembered the last time him and his son ate pizza together.

"Yeah!" Scar answered. "I think I want to try that pineapple pizza that shit look good."

"Yeah! You are going to love that." Broad Day Jay said, as he ordered a large pineapple pizza. "What you drinking?"

"A Snapple apple juice." Scar answered.

Broad Day Jay paid for the pizza and three Snapple Apple Juices. They found an empty table in the corner and sat down.

"So, what's up? I hear your name ringing back home." Broad Day Jay said, "every time I call home it's Scar this, Scar that."

"Is that a good or bad thing?" Scar asked looking Broad Day Jay in his eyes.

"A combination of both. The good are those who know you, knows you aren't a punk and won't go for just anything, but those who don't know you will try to go for theirs to get a rep off you."

"I don't worry about that." Scar said.

"I know, but you should worry about the police because once your name starts circulating in the air that's when they start to watch you closely. I know I had been under investigation for so many bodies that shit was starting to scare me. All they needed was for one to stick and then I'll be doing life in state prison. After years of wilding out I started to choose my moves more wisely and only use violence when the situation dictates. This day and time things are fucked up, there's cameras everywhere and it seems everything goes viral."

"You right, but drama keep coming to me. I be trying to chill but these niggas make a nigga carry the Tone. I stay strapped every day because I came too close to getting peeled. After I was shot, I took threats and warning signs seriously. I knew in order to get by I have to dead all beef before it starts." Scar said.

"Son, losing you is my top worry. I can't stomach anything happening to you, that shit will kill me. The years you spent in D.Y.S. were years that we were supposed to spend together. I never thought you would get all them years back then, but you did and while you were in, I began building this empire for us. Your Eighteen and I'm thirty-eight it's time to get your affairs in order. I spoke to your moms and she told me that when you first came home you were doing good, but then you started getting deeper and deeper in the streets. "What happened to you going to school? Is that still a dream of yours?

"Yeah! But like I told you I went on the run from D.Y.S. and then so much shit started happening I had to move one step ahead of everyone."

"So, do you still want to go? School is lovely up here with all these beautiful women running around." Uncle Stretch said trying to convince his son that Arizona is the best move for him.

"Yeah! I want to and I would love to live out here."

"I can arrange that." Uncle Stretch said.

"Alright let me straighten out a few things back home."

"When you go back home be safe." Uncle Stretch said.

"I refuse to let a nigga catch me slipping."

"You did let a nigga catch you slipping not once but twice."

Uncle Stretch said.

"What you mean twice," Broad Day Jay cut in.

Scar looked at Broad Day Jay and said, "I got into a couple situations with niggas from the hood and got popped twice. The only thing that saved me was the vest I was wearing."

"Damn, boy you know better than to be out there with no hammer on you." Broad Day Jay said.

"I did have my gun on me."

"Well, you need to be more on point out there in the streets. Who all you had situations with?"

"When I first came home, I was welcomed by everyone, but when I ran into the older head Free, we instantly bumped heads. I didn't know about the tension he had with my dad. I didn't take his threats seriously until the day me and him had the shoot-out."

"A shoot-out! When and where did all this happen?" Broad Day Jay asked.

"The night of Academy Day, I was cutting through the Four Squares and I saw Bully and he blammed at me and I returned the favor and hit him in the arm. I knew from that day it was on, but we didn't bump heads again until a few months later when they tried to ambush me on my way to St. Joe's."

"You said they. Who are they?"

"His crew. They sent this bitch to pop me, I peeped and hit her up, while I was blamming at her a nigga came around the corner busting at me and we got busy in the middle of the street. I backed him up then ran and hopped over a fence. As I was exerting in another clip a car rode up and shot me in the back. Luckily I had my vest on and it saved my life."

"So, all this was going on and you never thought about telling us?"
I didn't want to involve y'all in that situation. I was out there going for mine and if I felt like I couldn't handle it then I would have made the call. I had them niggas on edge."

"I understand that, but what if you would have had gotten killed that day, then what?" Broad Day Jay said seriously.

Scar didn't have an answer for that. What Broad Day Jay was saying was true and he knew he should have called them and told them all he was going through.

"You right. I should have told y'all. I guess I had trust in all the wrong niggas. While we were at Academy Day, I created a crew of niggas my age that we call the Wolf-Pack and we was supposed to watch each other's backs, but amongst the wolves we had a sheep. After Free got murked in Lynn his brother Sincere came home and I knew my problems with them niggas was far from over. I believe that Sincere manipulated this nigga name Rabbit to murk me because one day the nigga Rabbit told me he had some info on this kid from O.P. who I was after and when we got their Rabbit pulled out his gun and shot me a few times in the chest and ran."

"Damn, little nigga you were going through it back home. All this shit happened in the summer?"

"Yeah!"

"Where is this nigga Rabbit at now?" Broad Day Jay asked.

"In Nashua Street. After he shot me, he got in a police chase and got arrested with the gun that shot me."

"Did the police come and holler at you? What did you tell them?" Uncle Stretch asked.

"Nah! I had a vest on, so after I got shot, I dipped off and went home. I should bail his bitch ass out and murk him right outside of the county jail."

"Don't worry about that clown. He will get what's coming to him as soon as he touches the streets again." Broad Day Jay said.

"Son, I heard all that you went through and glad that you were honest. I brought you down here so all three of us can have a talk. I love you and if anything ever happened to you then it will be hell in Roxbury."

"I know and I'm trying to keep you from coming down to my aid. Dad, I can handle my own in these streets. I know how to move and each time I go through shit I learn from my mistakes and it makes me become more wiser."

"A mistake could cost you your life. I know many niggas who are not here today cause of mistakes they made." Uncle Stretch said.

"Dad, I know it was different back then. All these niggas be cyber beefing and shit. It's whack. That's why I won't take pictures because I refuse to let a nigga identify me on social media if you don't know what I look like then you don't. Most of these niggas are groupies too, so if we are beefing with O.P. and one of these other miscellaneous hoods want to get in good grace with O.P. and tell them what happened and then next thing you know they on Instagram taking pictures as a Collab for niggas it's crazy they be on that favor for a favor shit."

"What's a favor for a favor?" Broad Day Jay asked. "Is it the same as back in our day?"

"I don't know. That's this shit that these little niggas are on back home. A favor for a favor is say we cool with Castlegate and we having drama with someone they having drama with so we ask them to go do it for us and we'll do the same thing for them and no one will know who did it, but us."

"Okay. I see what's going on out there. I see the streets have changed." Uncle Stretch said.

"Yeah! They did I be hearing about all the stories on how niggas use to be getting money. Now all these little niggas care about is shooting or killing a nigga. These niggas be listening to all this gangsta music and try to impersonate what they hear. Don't get me wrong I listen to that gangsta shit too because they kick shit that I'm actually doing, but I don't let them motivate me to terrorize a nigga or his hood."

"So, it's hard to trust anyone these days back home." Broad Day Jay said.

"Trust shouldn't even be a word. I tried that shit when I created the Wolf Pack. I did that so that one could watch the other's back in time of need. That was a lesson well learned. I still got love for my niggas because one man's actions are not the actions of everyone." Scar said, as he spotted the waitress walking toward them with their order of pizza. "I will fill you in later to everything," Scar said, as the waitress placed the pizza on the table.

"Let's eat and show my little man all that Vegas has to offer." Uncle Stretch said.

After they finished eaten, they left the restaurant and walked inside an eye glass store called "Dolce". An older Caucasian sales lady saw them walk in and approached them.

"Good afternoon, may I help you with anything?"
The sales lady asked.
"Yes! I'm looking for the Cartier section."
"Follow me," The sales lady said, as she led them to the back of the store.

Uncle Stretch saw dozens of Cartier glasses in display cases. *"Damn, they got some official frames here."* Uncle Stretch thought, as he stared at the Cartier glasses.
"Are there any specific kind you are looking for sir?" The sales lady asked.
"Not really. I'm going to choose from your selection."
Uncle Stretch said.
"Okay. If you need any assistance can you, please let me know."
"Okay. Thank you. Shyheim, do you see anything you like?"

Uncle Stretch saw that his son had no clue about which ones he wanted, so he helped him and picked out a pair of wood frame Cartier's with light tint. The sales lady opened the display case and handed Scar the glasses. Scar tried on the glasses and saw how naturally they fit on his face.

"Yeah! These will do. What are these called?" Scar asked.
"Cartier's." Uncle Stretch answered, as he slid the sales lady his

American Express Card. The sales lady punched in the information and handed Uncle Stretch back his card. She completed the order, passed Scar the small bag and receipt.

"Thank you for shopping at Dolce." The sales lady said.

"You're welcome." Uncle Stretch said, as they turned around and left the store. They walked to the escalator and took it upstairs to the Grand Canal Mall. "Son, you're going to love this place it has everything in a mall, nice restaurants, night clubs, and a host of other things."

"I see this mall has all the exclusive stores. It reminds me of that mall in Natick." Scar said, as he followed his father inside the Gucci store. *"Damn, they got some pretty bitches in here"* Scar thought, as he eyed a couple females looking at purses.

"Welcome to Gucci, how may I help you today," a tall slim white salesman asked.

"I'm looking for something casual for my son."

"Is there anything specific that you are looking for sir?"

"A pair of dress pants, matching dress shirt and some shoes." Uncle Stretch said.

The salesman lead them to the section where the dress pants and shirts were located at. Scar looked through the racks and pulled out a tan pair of dress pants and saw a chocolate brown dress shirt and a matching blazer.

"Do you have any shoes that match this color?' Scar asked, as he pointed to the dress shirt.

"Yes!" The salesman said, "follow me," he walked over toward the section where the shoes and sneakers were located. He grabbed a pair of brown Gucci loafers and handed them to Scar.

"Oh yeah! These joints are fly. Do you have a size eleven?"

"Let me see. I'll be right back." The salesman said, as he walked to a back room.

Scar, Broad Day Jay and Uncle Stretch sat down on a bench and waited for the salesman to return. Scar saw how Broad Day Jay looked at him and asked.

"What's up Jay, why are you looking at me like that? What's on your mind?"

"I still can't believe how grown you had gotten. I know the bitches are loving you back home. How they are treating you?"

"Good. I can't complain." Scar smiled.

"Nigga are you getting pussy?" Broad Day Jay asked.

"Am I! I'm getting so much pussy that pussy should be my middle name," Scar laughed, "but yeah! I got a few dimes on my team. I have this older head out in Allston and this little Spanish mami in the South end."

"You haven't seen shit yet. These little bitches out west will put what we got back home to shame. Watch when we go to the club tonight."

"I already know the type of flavor they have out here. I been seeing nothing but eye candy since I been out here," Scar said, as he caught the eye of a petite Asian female. "Hold up Jay," Scar said, as he stood up and walked toward the female, "excuse me can I have a second of your time," Scar said to the female.

The female met Scar halfway and looked him up and down. She liked what she saw and smiled.

"How are you doing today?" Scar asked.

"I'm doing fine."

"Excuse me for not properly introducing myself, my name is Shyheim."

"Hi! Shyheim, my name is Naomie."

"Naomie, I saw you standing there and couldn't let you pass me by without acknowledging you and introducing myself."

"Aww! I knew I was special, but not that special," Naomie said, in a playful manner, "Shyheim, I see you have an accent where are you from?"

"Boston."

"Oh! The home of the New England Patriots."

"Yeah! The best of the best," Scar smiled. He looked and saw the salesman come from the back with a brown Gucci shoe box in his hand. "I don't mean to cut the conversation short, but I need to see if these loafers fit. Is it possible that we can exchange numbers and finish this conversation later?"

"Sure. We can do that," Naomie said, as she pulled out her phone and handed it to Scar. She watched Scar punch in his number, press send and hand it back to her. "Thank you, Shyheim. I look forward to finishing up this conversation."

"I should be thanking you for giving me the opportunity to get to know you. I'll call you."

"Please do." Naomie said, as she turned around and walked away.

"Damn, that's one bad bitch" Scar said, as he walked to where his father and Broad Day Jay was sitting.

"Pardon me, I couldn't let that one past me." Scar said as he sat down.

"I don't blame you." Broad Day Jay said.

The salesman opened the box, pulled out a loafer and handed it to Scar. Scar grabbed the loafer and tried it on.

"Yeah! It fits," Scar said, as he took the loafer off and passed it back to the salesman. They walked to the front counter and Uncle Stretch paid for the clothes and they left.

"I see you scored with that little pretty thang." Broad Day Jay said.

"What you thought I was playing. I told you my game is on one thousand." Scar boasted.

"I hear you little nigga. You took the first step in bagging her now let's see if you can move that bitch." Broad Day Jay said.

"Move. What you mean by that?" Scar asked perplexed.

"Son, anyone can get a bitch number or even fuck a bitch once they score, but it takes good game to move a bitch. When I say move a bitch, I mean by having a bitch do as you say, when you say and willing to make moves for you that she never made for no one else. Now, if you can't move a bitch then she is useless in your circle and then it's on to the next bitch."

"Oh! I get it."

"When you meet a female, you want to get to know the real them. You want to know them that no one else knows so when you get that little pretty Asian thang on the phone or behind closed doors interview that bitch," Uncle Stretch said, "You going to see that bitch again and it might be tonight at TAO, but when you do see that bitch make sure you got your game all the way turnt up. We still have a few hours before the club get lit. I wanted to get you right before we go out tonight so let me show you where your room is at," Uncle Stretch said, as he walked toward the escalator.

They took the escalator down to the main floor and walked toward a set of elevators. Uncle Stretch pressed a button and the elevator door popped open.

"Here son, this is the key to your room. The number is on the back. Call me if you need anything."

"Okay dad. Thanks."

"Remember what I said next time you see that bitch interview her because you never know what might come up out of that bitch."

You got that." Scar said, as he stepped on the elevator.

Chapter 50

"Damn, this spot is nice," Scar said, as he walked inside his hotel suite.

He placed his bags on the dresser and walked over to the bed and sat on it. He thought about what his father had told him about being able to move females. He knew what his father told him was true, by the way he was able to move Abby and have her do things that he wanted her to do. "Damn, I got a good bitch," Scar said as he leaned back on the bed and dozed off.

Three hours later Scar woke up and noticed he had a missed call from his father. As he started to dial his number a call came in. He

looked at the screen and saw his father's name and pressed the talk button.

"What's up pops?"

"You ready?"

"I just woke up. Give me a few to get myself in order."

"Alright. Clean yourself up and meet us at the same bar we met Jay at earlier."

"Got you." Scar said, as he ended the call. He dialed Abby's number to see what she was doing for the night.

* * * * * *

Abby decided to go out to a nightclub in Faneuil Hall with a few of her Boricua friends from the Villa Victoria Housing Project. The club was crowded with hundreds of people. Abby and her girls walked around the club seeing who was who and what was what. Abby spotted a group of niggas wearing Oakland Athletic caps in a corner by a set of speakers. She spotted Bully in the crowd and smiled.

Bully was leaning on a speaker blowing smoke in the air, disobeying the no smoking policy. The bouncers knew not to come near him because they would have to go through the thirty youngsters who surrounded him. Bully made sure each member of his crew had on Rest in Peace Sincere sweaters and Oakland Athletic Caps. Bully couldn't believe that Sincere was dead. He missed him dearly, but the loss of Sincere made Bully the boss of the Light Side of Academy Homes. Tonight, was his first night as boss and he was enjoying his new position. He knew he couldn't sleep well until Scar was dead. He wasn't 100% sure that Scar had killed Sincere, but he had an intuition it was him and with Scar missing in action, he figured his intuition was true.

Abby knew Bully had no clue who she was and if they did it would be hard to recognize her. She had dyed her hair brown. She traded her jeans and Jordan's in for a leather dress and a pair of Stuart Weitzman Shoes. Her designer shades covered her eyes. She felt her phone vibrate and looked at the screen saver and saw it was Scar. She pressed the talk button.

"Hey baby."

"What's up beautiful? Where you at? Sounds like you in a club."

"I am. Me and a few of my girls decided to go out to club Vertigo tonight."

"That's what's up. Are you enjoying yourself?

"Not like I would be if you were here. You know clubs aren't really my thing. I had to get out and enjoy myself."

"Make sure you make the best out of tonight. How is business?" Scar asked.

"Good. Our boy is holding it down."

"That's good to hear cause when I come home, I'm turning it up."

"I can't wait. I miss you."

"I miss you too."

"Baby, guess who's here?"

"Who?"

"Bully and a few of his friends."

"Oh yeah!"

"You should see the way he is acting. His ugly ass is feeling himself tonight."

"Fuck that fat fuck. Did he recognize you?"

"Nah! You know his ugly ass don't know me."

"I know, but you still have to watch him."

"I got my eye on his fat ass. How is your vacation?"

"It's good. I'm about to go and meet my pops. I wanted to call you before I head out."

"Thanks for calling. When are you coming back?"

"In a few weeks. It's nice out here you'll love it, next time I'm bringing you with me."

"Don't worry about me baby. I'll see you when you get back and enjoy your time with your dad. If I hear anything funny, I will let you know."

"Alright. I love you." Scar said.

"I love you more," Abby said, as she ended the call.

Abby looked at Bully and shook her head at how tough he was acting.

"Don't worry fat boy. There's a bullet with your name on it." Abby said.

Chapter 51

Scar walked to the bar and saw his father was wearing a heather Kiton Blazer, a grey and royal blue checkered cotton shirt and some matching grey trousers. He walked over to him. "What's up pops?" Scar said, as he gave his father a hug. "What's up Jay?" He said giving him threes.

Broad Day Jay was wearing a brown Lambskin jacket, a brown and grey cotton shirt and a pair of brown trousers. He had a grey silk scarf tied in a knot around his neck and a handcrafted woven straw hat on his head.

"Here this is your ticket into the club" Uncle Stretch said, as he passed Scar a V.I.P. Pass and a fake I.D.

Scar grabbed the fake I.D. and studied the information on it. "*Yeah, this will work.*" He thought, as he put the I.D, along with the V.I.P. Pass in his pocket.

"You got money for drinks?" Uncle Stretch asked.

"Yeah. I have a few hundos." Scar answered.

"That's pennies out here in Vegas." Uncle Stretch said, as he reached in his pocket and passed Scar a knot of 100's and 50's. "This is twenty-five hundred son. Do you. If you see something you like don't hesitate to ask her what she's drinking.

"Alright."

"Come on, let's get out of here and go and enjoy the night in style." Uncle Stretch said, as he led the way toward the escalators.

They walked over to the escalator and took it up to where Club Tao was located. They stepped off the escalator and walked to one of the two lines waiting to get into the club.

"Pops, why are there two lines?"

"One is for V.I.P. and the other is what I call the hope line."

"What's the hope line?" Scar asked.

"Son, the hope line are the people who are hoping to get in the club

"*Damn, Jay wasn't lying when he said these bitches out West are bad.*" Scar thought, as he kept walking.

As they walked inside the V.I.P. Area Scar felt someone grab his arm, as he went to shrug it off, he saw that it was the Asian female he had met earlier at the Gucci Store.

"Hi! Shyheim," Naomie said.

"What's up Naomie?" Scar said, as he gave her a hug.

"You look nice." Naomie said, as she complimented him on his dress code. "I see that blazer fits you well."

"I try my best to look the best" Scar said, as he eyed Naomie's outfit up and down. "You look like a million bucks in that gown. "I'm feeling your sexy look."

"Aww! Thank you, Shyheim, I'm glad that you are here maybe we can finish that conversation we had earlier a little later." Naomie said with a wink.

"Yeah! We can def finish that later."

"Well, I'm going to let you enjoy yourself and I'll catch you later." Naomie said.

"Damn, son who was that?" Uncle Stretch asked.

"That's the little thing that I met earlier at the Gucci store."

"Damn, that's her. All these Asian bitches look the same to me." Uncle Stretch said.

"You ain't lie about that dawg" Broad Day Jay said with a short giggle.

"I see that pretty thang got a nice ass on her." Broad Day Jay said, as he stared at how curvy her ass was. "You have to watch these bitches out here they be pros."

"Pros! What's a pro?" Scar asked.

"A pro is short for prostitute." Broad Day Jay informed.

"Oh! Alright."

They found a seat in the back of the V.I.P. Room and sat down. A few minutes later a bartender came up to their table and Uncle Stretch ordered three bottles of Dom Perignon. The next couple of hours Scar, his father and Broad Day Jay enjoyed their champagne and flirting with all the pretty girls in the V.I.P. Area.

A bartender was walking around the V.I.P. with a tray full of mini bottles of Rose Moet. Scar picked one up from the tray, paid for it and popped the cork. He took and long gulp.

"Sharing?" A female voice asked.

Scar turned and saw Naomie standing there with a smile on her face.

"Yeah Why not." Scar said, as he passed her the champagne.

"Are you ready to go and finish that conversation?" Naomie said with a smile on her face.

"Yeah! We can do that." Scar said.

"I think we should go somewhere less quiet." Naomie said with a wink.

"Alright. Hold on let me tell my peeps I'm leaving." Scar said, as he walked over to his father and Broad Day Jay. "I'm about to dip off with this pretty bitch and bring the New Year in right. I'll get up with y'all in the A.M." Scar said, as he gave both of them threes and walked over to Naomie and wrapped his arms around her neck and walked out of the club. They flirted the whole time until they reached Scar's hotel suite. They walked in the suite and Naomie saw a wall size mirror and headed over to it and began fixing her hair.

"I don't know why you are doing all that it's going to get messed up anyways." Scar said jokingly.

"Says who!" Naomie said, as she placed her hands on her hips. She walked over to the bed and sat on the edge. "So, Shyheim tell me a few things about you."

"What do you want to know?"

"Whatever you want to tell me." Naomie giggled.

"You know my name, where I'm from and my age. What else do you want to know?"

"Well, what brought you to Vegas?"

"My father been living on the West Coast for close to ten years and I wanted to spend some time with him."

"Was one of the guys with you your father?"

"Yeah! The one who had on the light grey blazer."

"I figured that. When I first saw y'all in the Gucci store I thought he was your brother."

"Yeah! Everyone thinks that, but that's my old man. So, what about you, where are you from?"

"Originally, I'm from San Francisco, but my job kept me commuting back and forth quite often."

"Sounds like your job keeps you busy."

"It does, but it pays the bills and at the end that's all that matters."

"I hear that. Do you have any kids?"

"No!" Naomie answered. "What about you?"

"Nah!"

"That's good to know it seem like these days all men have kids."

"Nuff of that small talk let me see what those curves look like."

"What I look like some easy fuck? I should be charging you for what we are about to do, but you are cute so I'm going to give you a pass." Naomie said, as she began un-strapping her red bottoms.

"Charging me. I should be charging you." Scar shot back with a giggle.

"No! Honey, I'm serious in my profession it's pay for play."

"What profession is that?" Scar asked confused.

"I'm a call girl."

"*Damn, this bitch tricked me.*" Scar thought, as he felt like a fool for bringing a prostitute to his hotel suite. "*Fuck it, what's done is done.*" He thought. "Well, let's make this night special."

"Now that's a conversation I was talking about." Naomie said, as she took off her shoes, stepped up and lifted her gown over her head.

"*Damn, this pretty bitch had no panties on all night.*" Scar thought, as his dick became hard as a brick.

Scar took off his clothes and grabbed a condom out of the dresser, opened it with his teeth and rolled it on his dick. As Scar was putting on the condom Naomie turned around and held onto the edge of the bed giving Scar a perfect view of her round booty. Scar walked up to her, grabbed her waist and inserted his dick in her opening. As he started stroking, she started meeting his stroke wit strokes of her own. Scar was loving this as he never had someone throw it back on him.

After they both cummed he pulled out and grabbed another condom. As he changed condoms she combed on the bed and started playing with her clit. He climbed on the bed and grabbed her legs and lifted them. She wrapped them around his waist and lifted her body slightly upward. This position gave Scar a direct pussy shot. He started pumping fast in an attempt to knock the bottom of her pussy out. He cummed for the second time. She unwrapped her legs and grabbed his dick, pulled off the condom and tossed it in the corner. He laid on the bed and she crawled between his legs and placed his balls in her mouth and started sucking them while left hand stroked the shaft of his dick. Within minutes Scar cummed for the third time. She kept jerking his dick with her mouth from his balls and licked the cum off of her fingers and smiled at him. "How you like that daddy?"

"No comment." Scar laughed, as he watched her place her lips around the head of his dick. She contracted her cheek muscles and gave Scar the best head he ever received. After she finished sucking his dick, she got up and walked to the bathroom to clean herself up. When she came back Scar was sound asleep. She tossed on her clothes, grabbed a pen and wrote a note on the back of one of her business cards, placed it on the dresser and left.

The next morning Scar woke up and saw that Naomie was gone. He rose from the bed and saw that she had left a business card on the dresser and saw that it a note on the back. He read the note.

"We had an amazing night. Thanks for the time we spent cutie. I'm sorry I couldn't be there when you wake up, but I had to skip out on you because I have some business to attend to. Next time you come into town look me up.

XOXO Naomie."

"Wow, what a night. Wait till I tell my pops about this." Scar said, as he walked to the bathroom to take a shower.

Chapter 52

Scar took a shower and got dressed. He walked to the living room area of his suite and picked up his phone from the coffee table and saw he had a missed call from his father. He scrolled to his father's number and tapped the touch screen. After a couple rings Uncle Stretch picked up.

"What's up pops?"

"How was your night?"

"It went well, but you are not going to believe what I have to tell you about ole girl."

"What? Talk to me."

"Everything was going smooth and before we got to business, she told me that she was working as a call girl."

"What are you surprised?"

"Yeah! I wasn't expecting that."

"Me and Jay told you to watch these bitches out here. Most of these bitches be out here selling their ass for cash. So, what happened? Did you pay for play?"

"Fuck no! She told me all this bullshit about she should charge me, but she was giving me a pass because I was cute."

"Oh! So, in other words she used you for some free dick, that's when you were supposed to reverse that and tell her that your dick costs. Was it a good fuck?"

"Yeah! The bitch gives a mean head job and is a beast in the sheets."

"So, long as you handled your business that's all that matters. What you want to do today?"

"I'm with you. It's your call. I'm just ready to enjoy my last day before I head back home."

"I want to take you to this mall next to Caesars Palace. You are going to love it. There's no place like it. When you ready meet me at the entryway of the mall.

"Alright, give me a few and I'll be right down." Scar said, as he hung up the phone.

Twenty minutes later Scar made his way to the mall and saw his father talking to Broad Day Jay next to some benches. He walked over and gave them a hug.

"What's up boy? I hear you had a great time last night." Broad Day

344

Jay said.

"Yeah! The night went well. I thought I met something official turned out to be a hoe."

"It happens. At Least you had a good time and got a piece of free ass."

"True. It was crazy cause when I woke up, I saw a note on the dresser that said next time I'm in town call her." Scar said, as he followed them through the mall.

"That's Vegas for you."

They walked through the mall and turned into the Madame Tussaud Wax museum.

"Damn, there's a lot of celebrities here," Scar said, as he thought he saw Kim Kardashian talking to Paris Hilton. He walked closer and stared at Kim Kardashian's ass. *"Damn, I can't believe I'm face to face with this bitch."* Scar thought.

"Son, what are you staring at?" Uncle Stretch asked.

"Kim-K." Scar responded.

"That's not her. We are in a wax museum." Uncle Stretch laughed.

Scar looked closer and saw that none of the celebrities were moving and shook his head. "Damn, I'm bugging. I must still be tired" Scar said, with a laugh of his own. "What is this place called?"

"The Madame Tussaud Wax Museum." Broad Day Jay informed.

"Are you hungry?"

"Yeah! I didn't eat anything since last night."

"What you have a taste for?" Uncle Stretch asked.

"A burger." Scar replied.

"I know the perfect place," Broad Day Jay said, as they walked out of the wax museum.

"After we eat, we are going to go shopping at the mall I was telling you about."

"Alright." Scar said, as he followed his father and Broad Day Jay through the mall.

Broad Day Jay led the way toward B&B Burger and Beer Restaurant. They walked in and saw an empty table and sat down.

"You have to test these grilled onion turkey burgers they have." Broad Day Jay said.

"I'll test it. What kind of sides do they have?" Scar asked.

"You have to get the beer battered onion rings."

Broad Day Jay answered.

"Alright." Scar said, as he saw a waitress walking over to their table.

"How you doing today gentlemen? How may I help you?"

"I would like two orders of your onion turkey burgers and a side of beer battered onion rings." Broad Day Jay answered.

"Is that it sir?"

"What you are drinking?" Broad Day Jay asked Scar.

Broad Day Jay noticed that Scar was confused and ordered two bottles of Becks. One for him and the other for Scar.

"Pops, you not going to eat?"

"I ate earlier, plus I don't eat too much fast food because it's not good for your health. I am real conscious of what and when I eat. It's called eating to live son. I have a regimen where I eat something light in the morning and the afternoon hours and then I eat a full course meal a day between four to six in the evening.'

"Damn, you don't be hungry eating like that?" Scar asked.

"No. I'm used to it now. I have been doing this for the past six years. It's called discipline."

"Discipline my ass. It's called starvation." Broad Day Jay joked. "So, what's your plans when you leave here?" He asked Scar.

"I'm going to spend a few days with my girl and then I'm back to the money." Scar answered.

"Be careful back home. My sister told me earlier that they had a special on the news about hot spots in Boston and our hood was the number one hot spot in the city."

"Word, that's not good." Scar said.

"I know. So do your best to stay away from the hood for a little while until it cools down." Broad Day Jay said looking Scar in the eyes, "plus with all the shit you discussed with us you don't know who to trust."

"I hope you are taking into consideration about making that move down here with me." Uncle Stretch said looking at his son.

"I am definitely considering it. Let me tie up all my loose ends and I will get back to you on the move down here. To be honest pops, I don't like the idea of leaving my girl back home."

'Who said you have to leave her." Uncle Stretch said.

"Alright. I will talk to her about it when I get back."

"How much money do you have stacked?"

"It should be a little over one hundred racks. If I come down here with money can you help me invest it?"

"Of course I would, I told you to bring all the money you have back home, and I will show you how to invest that dirty money into rental properties. Matter of fact, what you bring to the table I will match it dollar for dollar."

"Now, that's what I'm talking about." Scar said, as he saw the waitress walking toward him with two plates in her hand.

The waitress placed a plate in front of Scar and Broad Day Jay. Scar picked up his burger and bit into it. He looked at his father and saw how clear his skin was and wondered if it came from his eating habits. After they finished in the restaurant they left and walked outside.

Uncle Stretch walked toward the valet and said a few words to him. The valet disappeared and a few minutes later returned driving Uncle Stretch's BMW. He stepped out and shook Uncle Stretch's hand and walked away. They all got in the BMW and drove off toward the Las Vegas Strip. Uncle Stretch turned up the volume and sung word for word to the song "30-Something" by Jay-Z.

"I already know what you want me to do/ I did all that by the age of twenty-one/ by twenty-two/ I had that brand new AC coupe/ I guess you can say my legend had just begun/ I'm young enough to know the right car to buy and grown enough to not put rims on it."

Scar sat in the backseat listening to his father swap verse for verse with Jay-Z. He looked out the window at all the casinos that lined the strip. He was amazed at how exclusive some of the designs of the casinos was.

Uncle Stretch rode past Caesars Palace and pulled into the parking lot of the Forum shopping mall. He parked and took the key out of the ignition and stepped out.

Scar stepped out and was amazed at how many pretty women were going in and out of the mall.

"Son, this is one of the best malls in the country. There be so many bad bitches here. You will see," Uncle Stretch said, as he walked toward the mall entrance.

The next three hours Scar managed to rack up over a half dozen numbers from some of the prettiest females his eyes ever graced. He was loving Vegas and was starting to think twice about bringing Abby with him.

"Nah! I can't do that to her. She did some shit for me that no other bitch would do." Scar thought, as he pushed a carriage that was filled with bags of clothes that his father had bought him.

After they finished shopping, they went back to the Venetian and spent a few hours at the Canyon Ranch Spa Club. There Scar got a massage, facial and a manicure and pedicure.

"Son, I hope you enjoyed yourself out here with me and really consider making that move out here. There's so much to offer, you'll be a fool to stay back home."

"I got you pops, let me just handle what needs to be handled and I'll be on my way back."

"Now, that's what I wanted to hear." Uncle Stretch said, as he hugged his son.

Chapter 53

Uncle Stretch taught his son a little about investing in the financial market and took him through a crash course in the real estate market for the next month. Scar was appreciative of all that his father taught him and done for him during his stay out west. The day Scar was set to leave he woke up at 4:45 am and walked downstairs to the dining room and saw his father reading the Wall Street Journal. He walked up to his dad and gave him a hug.

"What's up dad?" Scar said, as he saw that his father had the T.V. on a business station. "What you watching?"

"Bloomberg. It's a financial station. They cover everything regarding the financial and business markets. After I drop you off, I'm going to watch the market and put in a few trades in the option market."

"I hear that. When I come back, maybe you can teach me that when I come back."

"No problem son. Whatever knowledge I have is yours. I had a great time out here with you, do what you gotta do back home and come back and live like a king."

"I got you." Scar said, as he walked to the kitchen and made himself some breakfast.

After Scar ate his breakfast they left and went to the airport. Scar gave his father a hug, grabbed his luggage and walked inside the airport. *"In umpteen hours I will be back in the bean."* Scar said to himself. Scar boarded the plane, took his seat and dozed off. He woke up six hours later and was amazed that he was still on the plane. *"Damn, this is a long ass plane ride."* Scar grabbed his iPod and started to listen to music for the remainder of the plane ride. He saw the plane slowing down and knew it was about to land. *"About time."* The plane landed at Boston Logan International Airport and Scar stepped off and followed the crowd through the terminal. He walked to the baggage claim picked up his luggage and walked out of the airport. "Home sweet home." Scar said, as he walked to a taxi stand.

Scar placed his luggage in the trunk of a taxi, opened the rear door and inched himself into the backseat. "Cathedral Project," Scar said directing the driver to Abby's apartment. He sat in the back seat and thought about all that he had experienced during his trip. *"What happens in Vegas stays in Vegas,"* Scar said, as he thought about his night with Naomie.

The taxi pulled up outside of Abby's building. Scar paid the fare and gave the driver a tip. He exited the taxi, grabbed his luggage and headed toward Abby's apartment. He walked upstairs and used his key to enter.

Abby was sitting on the couch watching television in a pair of shorts and a tank top when she heard a key fiddling in the key hole. She stood up and walked to the door just as Scar walked in. He placed his luggage on the side of the door and walked toward Abby.

"What's up girl?"

"Hey baby, I been missing you." Abby replied, as she ran over to Scar and gave him a flurry of kisses all over his face. "I thought you were coming back in January."

"I was, but I couldn't be away from you any longer. I spent Thanksgiving down there with my dad. We didn't celebrate it for our culture beliefs. Did you miss me?" Scar asked.

"Did I miss you. What kind of question is that? Of course, I missed your crazy ass. How was your Thanksgiving?"

"Me and my pops don't celebrate that holiday or any other pagan holiday."

"Oh! I forgot about your way of life. How was your trip?"

"Great. My dad is literally rich. He owns businesses and real estate in Nevada and Arizona. He showed me a few houses he owned out there, but the best part of the trip besides our long talks was when we went to Vegas to see my godfather. Baby, Vegas is unbelievable we have to go there."

"Wow. It sounds like you had a blast."

"I did. He offered to help us invest our dirty money into a legitimate means of income."

"What legit ways did y'all discuss'?"

"Real estate, investing in the financial market and open up small businesses. He told me the best way to clean dirty money is through the real estate game. He broke down ways how to do it through using bank money to clean our money."

"Sounds like he knows what he is talking about."

"Do he. He owns a real estate company, several rental properties and a rental management company called "Academy Rentals". He wanted me to move down there so he can show me the game."

"What you tell him?"

"I told him the only way I will make the move is if I bring my lady with me."

"What he say about that?"

"He said he has enough room for the both of us."

"Do you think that will be a good move for us with all the money that we are making here?"

"We need to create an exit plan and figure out what we are going to do with this money that we are making. It's never good to have money sit idle. We can invest our money, relax and start a family."

"A family NIGGA! I don't want no kids by you." Abby said with a smile on her face.

"Well if you don't then there are others who would love to have a family by me."

"Nigga, you know I want your kids. I'm glad you had a good time and made it back safe. While you were gone Jose made us an easy thirty thousand profit. Let's make a few more runs and then we can explore that option that your father is speaking about."

"What have I missed in these streets?"

"Nothing. It's been quiet. I already told you that I saw the nigga Bully at the club. You should of saw how his fat ass was acting. You know the word on the street is that he put out a ten thou price tag up for anyone who knows who killed Sincere."

"How do you know that?"

"You know Kia's my girl."

"Damn, baby you should have told him who did it and collected the ten gees and murked him." Scar said jokingly, "fuck that fat fuck. He's next on the list." Scar said seriously.

"Baby can I do it. I would enjoy watching his fat ass squeal like a pig."

"Nah! I want to complete the trifecta." Scar said, as he thought about how he killed Free and Sincere.

"What you mean trifecta?"

"Use your imagination."

Scar knew Abby had no clue about who had killed Free or the depths of his and Scar's beef. The only two people who knew that he had killed Free was his father and Broad Day Jay. He felt his phone vibrate in his pocket, he reached in it and pulled it out and saw that it was his mother.

"What's up ma?"

"How you enjoying your trip?"

"It went well. I came back an hour ago. Once I get finished spending time with my girl then I am coming by to spend some time with you."

"I'm glad that you made it home safely. What did y'all do out there?"

"A lot. He taught me a few things about real estate and investing. So, the trip definitely served its purpose. Then we went to Vegas and saw Jay."

"Sounds like you had a good time."

"Every time I see my dad, I have a good time. We even talked about the possibility of me moving down there to live with him."

"That will be a great move for you. You need to be with him and leave these streets alone. There's nothing out in these streets for you. These streets are getting worse every day."

"I know it's nothing out here for me and that's why I'm going to make that move out west." Scar said, as he thought about all the people, he was responsible for killing. "I will stop by tomorrow so we can talk. I love you."

"I love you too." Baby Fe said, "tell your girl I said hello."

"My mom said hello."

"Oh, next time you speak or see her tell her I said hello. Oh yeah, Kia, told me to tell you that since Sincere's death they moved the show from January the third to two days before Christmas."

"Damn, that's in a few days. I might show up there and hear a few of my niggas from the Gate rock the mic."

"Fuck that, my pussy is itching. I need some of that dick." Abby said, as she pulled down her shorts to reveal she had on no panties. "You ready to catch up on what you missed papi?"

"Now, that's what I'm talking about," Scar said, as he took off his clothes and watched as Abby took off her tank top and shorts.

Chapter 54

Tay pulled into the parking lot of Club Roxy in Providence, Rhode Island. She parked beside a white Jaguar and stepped out. She walked inside the club in a red and white Vera Wang dress and white Christian Louboutin red bottom shoes. Her ass was so fat that everyone who knew her thought she had a butt implant.

"Tay boogie, what's up," Dave Dollar said, as she examined how thick she had gotten.

"Long time no see," Tay said, as she saw how stylish he was.

Tay hadn't seen Dave Dollar in over a decade and was glad that he still was that nigga he'd always been. She was so busy organizing all the movements that she was part of that she had left the streets and those involved with alone.

"How is your family?" Tay asked.

"They are alright. Everyone is doing great. My son, Lil Davey is around here somewhere. How are your sons?"

"They are good." Tay replied.

"If they need anything let me know." Dave Dollar said.

"They are good. Thanks anyways."

"We gotta take some pictures," Dave Dollar said, as he led the way over to the photo area.

Tay watched as he handed the photographer a hundred-dollar bill. Tay took all types of pictures with him. Dave Dollar passed her six out of the ten pictures, hugged her and walked away.

Tay walked over to where her crew was posted. She gave hugs and kisses to each and every one of them. Tay listened to all the street tales that her girls spoke about. She couldn't believe all the stuff she had missed. She pulled out her cell phone and texted her sister. A few seconds later Baby Fe texted back.

"Have you met Noodles?" Tay's friend Kay-Kay asked.

"Not yet. Is she here?"

"Yeah! She's right there?" Brown Eyes pointed.

Tay looked and spotted a beautiful Asian looking female walking toward them. Noodles had on red jeans, a red and white Roberto Cavalli Shirt, and some matching shoes. Her fingernails were painted red with white swirls.

"She's pretty," Tay thought, as she stared at Noodles, "Hey, what's up Noodles? My name is Tay."

"Heyyy, it's finally nice to meet you. I have been hearing a lot about you." Noodles said, as she gave Tay a hug.

"You look like that actress Karruche Tran," Tay commented.

Noodles chuckled because everyone be mistaken her for the actress. "Thank you. I'll take that as a compliment."

Noodles introduced her team of girls to the elders and they partied, drank champagne, and waited for the show to begin.

"Tay, there goes your sister," Kay Kay pointed.

Baby Fe walked over with a clear bottle of Rose Moet in her hand. She had on a pair of white and blue Todd sneakers, blue dress pants and a white blouse.

Bully eyes scanned the club as he made his way through the crowd. He had in his pocket a .380 Beretta loaded with Hollow tip bullets. He planned to give Scar all eight to the face. He saw Pitt and walked over.

"What's good, Pitt. I see the whole squad is here. I wish Sincere was here to see this. He would have loved it."

"I know. He was one of the niggas who had put this whole thing together." Pitt said.

"Is the whole Wolf Pack here?" Bully asked, as he looked around to

362

see if he could spot Scar.

"I just came in. I'm not sure who's here dawg, but I know it's all family though.

Bully nodded, gave dap to Pitt and walked around the club. He looked feverishly for Scar.

* * * * * *

Scar was sitting in Kia's apartment talking to her about the time he had spent in Arizona with his father and how he had decided to move there. He was still in disbelief that Rabbit went against the grain and fucked up his last bullet-proof vest. That was the second time he had gotten shot, wearing a vest and he vowed to never let anyone get that close to him.

While Scar was in Kia's apartment, a black van came to a stop at Ritchie Street. The door slid open, Mud stepped out, and walked into the project. The van pulled off and stopped at Academy Court and Nastee hopped out cradling an MP5 submachine gun in his arms. The van pulled off and stopped at Dimock Street in the Four Squares. Terrible Trav hopped out with a six shot 12-Gauge shotgun in his hand and .357 automatic handgun in his waist. The three killers canvassed the project looking for people to savagely murder.

Mud continued his journey into the project. His alert eyes took inventory of everything on the street. He clutched a Heckler & Koch

P87 handgun. He turned on Weaver Way and saw Nastee walking up Academy Court. Mud still remembered his last encounter in the project. It didn't go as he planned it and he would be damned if history repeated itself. "*Where the fuck is everyone at?*" Mud thought, as he saw there was not a soul inside the housing project.

Scar walked out of Kia's apartment and spotted someone limping down the street. His gut told him that it was immediate danger. He looked closer and saw that the person had in his hand a big handgun. Scar walked behind a dumpster and hid.

Mud slowed his pace as he spotted a group congregating near an abandoned car. He raised his pistol and fired. The crack heads ducked and scattered like roaches down the steps that led to Slayton Way. Mud followed them, walked into the hallway and up the stairs. He looked out the window at the bus stop, and saw a couple youngsters with Atlanta Braves Caps and Coats talking to females. Mud stuck the gun out of the window and fired into the crowd. He struck a few, backed away, and exited the hallway.

Nastee's pursuit of Scar led him to chokeslam Baby Fe. He never wanted to kill anyone bad as he wanted to kill Scar. "This bastard killed both of my sons, when I catch him, I will riddle his face and detach it from the rest of his body."

Tonight, Nastee was determined to kill Scar. He scanned roof-tops, and project hallways for signs of Atlanta Braves caps. Wasn't nothing stopping him. Not even the police. If they pulled up they would be backed down by high powered bullets that would slice their Kevlar vests.

Scar heard the gunshots and kept his eyes fixated on another person walking with a gun.

"Damn, they are everywhere," Scar said, as he continued to hide behind a dumpster.

Scar ran to the woods. He knew as long as he stayed in the woods, he would win the shoot-out. He walked over to a log, lifted it and reached in a hole. He replaced his handgun for a Mac-10. He walked over to a tree and hid behind it. He saw Terrible Trav walk past the woods with a shotgun in his hand. Scar raised the Mac-10 and pulled the trigger. The .45 bullets sputtered out of the Mac-10 and hit Terrible Trav in his back.

Mud heard the shots and turned the corner. Scar pointed the Mac-10 and pulled the trigger. The .45 bullets spit at Mud and missed him as he ducked and ran behind a car.

Mud raised the P87 and fired into the woods. Nastee heard the exchange of gunfire and wanted to join the fun. He aimed the MP5 at the woods and pulled the trigger. The flurry of gunshots had Scar running for his life. Mud raised his gun and fired more rounds into the woods. The clip fell out and he replaced it with another one.

Scar ran behind a dumpster, spun around, and was face to face with
Nastee. Scar raised his Mac-10 and pulled the trigger. A hail of bullets
flew from the Mac and danced into Nastee's chest. His large frame
stumbled backward and hit the pavement with a thump. Scar ran up
on him, looked him in the eye and said. "I won," and shot Nastee a
few more times.

Nastee died with his eyes open to the man who was responsible for
the death of both of his sons. Scar was so preoccupied with killing
Nastee that he forgot about Mud. Scar turned, saw Mud coming
toward him and tried to run. Mud already had his gun raised and pulled
the trigger. The first shot hit Scar in his shoulder and spun his body
around. The next two hit him in his left arm and hip. He hopped away
as the fourth shot hit him in his back and knocked him off his feet. He
crawled behind a dumpster leaving the Mac-10 on the ground as blood
leaked from the holes in his body.

Mud heard sirens coming, ran past Nastee and Terrible Trav's lifeless
bodies, and made his way through the project. He hopped in the
getaway van and pulled off.

Kia heard the exchange of gunfire and looked out her window. She
saw someone crawl behind a dumpster. She waited for a few minutes
and stepped out. She saw Nastee and Terrible Trav on the ground dead
and a Mac-10 near a dumpster. She looked behind the dumpster and
saw Scar gurgling blood. "OH! SHIT! SCAR! SCAR!" She said
frantically, as she heard the sirens coming. She picked up the Mac-10

and ran back into the house and called Pitt.

Chapter 55

Tay watched as the curtain opened and a gigantic Cincinnati Reds sign appeared. A stripper pole was on the right side of the stage in a V.I.P. Section. She saw Trigga and two of the prettiest females she had ever seen, sitting in the V.I.P. surrounded by dozens of bottles of Rose Moet.

"THIS IS IT! ROXY, THROW YOUR HANDS UP! THROW YOUR HANDS UP!" Nice shouted.

The whole crowd went crazy throwing three fingers in the air in honor of the Boston three finger salute. Ratface Gremlin came out with a bottle of Rose Moet, rhyming words to his song "Rosey Moe." Tay watched as the girls fondled Trigga on the couch. The crowd got hyped as they watched the show that Ratface Gremlin put on. He finished his set and stepped off the stage. Diamond Handz stepped out rhyming his hood anthem "Alphabet Heaven." Where he named all the niggas from his hood through the 26 letters of the alphabet in rhythm.

Tay started doing the C.G.G. (Castlegate Girls) stomp with her little sister. The lights dimmed as a few strippers came out and started dancing as Diamond Handz rhymed his ode to the strippers.

Bully was becoming frustrated by the minute as he searched for Scar throughout the club. *"Where the fuck is this nigga at?"* Bully thought.

Midway through the show, Pitt stepped to Baby Fe and pulled her to the side. "I need to talk to you. I just spoke to my girlfriend and she told me that a couple people got shot and one of them was your son, Scar."

Baby Fe screamed and dropped to her knees. Pitt pulled her up and hugged her. She looked into Pitt's eyes and asked. "Are you sure?"

Pitt nodded his head and they walked over to where Tay was standing. Bully saw Pitt, Baby Fe and Tay huddled and walked over toward them. As he neared them, he overheard Baby Fe tell her sister that Scar had gotten shot in Academy. He backed up and kept his distance and watched as Tay handed her car keys to one of her friends and left.

"Damn, I hope this little nigga don't die. I want to be the one who put

him in the dirt," Bully said to himself, as he followed them out of the club, "*I'm going to meet them in the project and see for my own eyes.*

Bully sped to Boston like he was racing in the Indianapolis 500. He made it to the project in twenty minutes and parked on the Light Side. He walked down the hill and saw dozens of police cruisers, ambulances and coroner trucks parked. "*What the fuck happened?* He wondered, as he stood across the street watching the gang-unit, homicide unit, and other detectives talk to a few people standing around. "*I need to know what happened?*" He thought, as he crossed the street. He walked over to a few residents of the Dark Side and slid beside them.

"Hey, Billy." An older lady named Dina said, as she hugged and kissed him.
"What happened?" Billy asked.
"I don't know. I just heard a lot of gunshots and called the police. I came out here and right there on Columbus Ave a couple people got shot" the lady said pointing, "then over on Academy Road a couple people got shot."
"*Damn, this nigga might really be dead.*" Bully said, as he saw Baby Fe's car.

Baby Fe pulled up to the Dark Side and parked. The entrance of the project was taped off in yellow caution tape. Tay broke down from the sight of the coroner trucks that were parked in strategic places. She walked over to where the detectives were standing. She tried to lift the

371

yellow caution tape but was stopped by a detective.

"EXCUSE ME MISS, THIS IS A HOMICIDE INVESTIGATION."
The detective said.
"GET THE FUCK OFF OF ME! GET THE FUCK OFF OF ME!
THAT'S MY SON!" Baby Fe yelled.
"Hold on miss," the detective said.
"GO GET MR. STERNER." Baby Fe demanded.

The officer radioed for Mr. Sterner. Minutes later Mr. Homicide came
down and saw Tay and Baby Fe.

"Can I help you? What's the problem?" Mr. Homicide asked politely.
Tay looked at the homicide detective and resisted the urge to spit in
his face.

"MY SON IS OVER THERE DEAD!" Baby Fe shouted, to a body
under a white sheet, "AND HE WON'T LET ME IN TO SEE MY
SON." She yelled, as she began to climb under the yellow tape.

One of the detectives was ready to grab Baby Fe's arm and looked at
Mr. Homicide.

"Let them through. I got this." Mr. Homicide said.

Mr. Homicide walked both sisters inside the housing project and
stopped at a white sheet. He bent down, lifted the white sheet and

looked up at the sisters. What Tay saw made her cry as she stared at Nastee dead with his eyes open.

Tay's tears were for all the good times she shared with Nastee, the loss of their son and the fact that she would never see him alive again. She wiped away the tears and hoped that her nephew was not one of the victims.

Baby Fe saw Nastee's body and cocked back a mouth full of spit and spat in Nastee's face. Mr. Homicide grabbed her and picked her up. She tussled with him as he brought her near a dumpster and put her down.
"Don't do that again or you're going to jail," Mr. Homicide warned her. "Follow me." He said as he led her to the dumpsters.

Baby Fe followed the detective and saw a trail of blood leading to the back of the dumpster. She continued to follow the detective and what she saw made her scream at the top of her lungs. "NOOOOOO!"

Scar was laid in a fetal position, surrounded in a pool of his own blood. Mr. Homicide stood there and watched Baby Fe's reaction. He wanted to laugh but he didn't.
"I knew this was going to happen. I saw this outcome hundreds of times with these young street punks." Mr. Homicide said to himself."

As tears streamed down Baby Fe's face, she thought about all the memories she had with her son, the day he came home from the youth center and how he was about to enter a new phase of his life. She couldn't believe that she had lost him to the streets of Boston. Her sister came up to her and embraced her with a hug.

Tay knew the streets were cold. She closed her eyes and said a quick prayer. As she closed her eyes a few faces flashed through her mind: Casino Mike, her older brother Ramel and her brother's friends from her hood. *"Damn, if my brother was alive things would have been different, none of this would have had happened."* Tay thought as tears streamed down her face as she opened her eyes and held her sister tightly.

Made in the USA
Middletown, DE
29 September 2024

61322430R00215